OCT   2017

WATCHDOG

ALSO BY WILL McINTOSH

Burning Midnight

WATCHDOG

WILL McINTOSH

Delacorte Press

Text copyright © 2017 by Will McIntosh
Jacket art copyright © 2017 by M. S. Corley

Delacorte Press is a registered trademark and the colophon is a trademark of Penguin Random House LLC.

Visit us on the Web! randomhousekids.com

Educators and librarians, for a variety of teaching tools, visit us at RHTeachersLibrarians.com

Library of Congress Cataloging-in-Publication Data
Names: McIntosh, Will, author.
Title: Watchdog / Will McIntosh.
Description: First edition. | New York : Delacorte Press, [2017]
Summary: Orphaned and homeless, fourteen-year-old twins Vick and Tara, who is autistic, go up against a crime lord and her four-legged robotic army, with help from their robotic dog, Daisy.
Identifiers: LCCN 2016049554 (print) | LCCN 2017022938 (ebook)
| ISBN 978-1-5247-1385-0 (el) | ISBN 978-1-5247-1384-3 (hc) |
ISBN 978-1-5247-1386-7 (glb)
Subjects: | CYAC: Homeless persons—Fiction. | Brothers and sisters—Fiction. | Twins—Fiction. | Robots—Fiction. | Criminals—Fiction. | Autism—Fiction. | Orphans—Fiction. | Science fiction. | BISAC: JUVENILE FICTION / Robots. | JUVENILE FICTION / Animals / Dogs. | JUVENILE FICTION / Action & Adventure / General.
Classification: LCC PZ7.1.M4353 (ebook) | LCC PZ7.1.M4353 Wat 2017 (print) | DDC [Fic]—dc23

The text of this book is set in 13-point Minion Pro.
Interior design by Ken Crossland

Printed in the United States of America
10 9 8 7 6 5 4 3 2 1
First Edition

For my twins, Hannah and Miles,
who will be just about old enough
to read this book when it comes out

CHAPTER 1

Vick never got used to the smell. Usually he stopped noticing bad smells after a while, but the eye-watering stink of mountains of trash baking in the blazing August sun was so bad, it made every breath an ordeal. And then there were the flies buzzing around Vick's face, landing on him with their tickly legs. He never got used to them, either.

Vick plunged his hand into the hole he was digging in the mountain of cardboard, plastic, dirty diapers, rotting bits of meat, used coffee filters, old socks, sticky wrappers, and unidentifiable sludge. There were already holes in the gloves he'd bought last week, so his bare fingertips were covered in filth he didn't even want to think about. His back ached.

It wasn't even noon yet. Still hours to go.

His fingers brushed something hard and metallic. Vick dug faster, widening the hole. By now he could tell immediately when he'd struck something with potential. Tossing handfuls of trash aside, he exposed a blood-red tube. He tugged it free, then brushed crud off of it.

It was L-shaped, with fine wires trailing out of one end. He held it up and looked around for his twin sister. "Tara? Is this any good?"

Vick scanned the dump, which stretched for three blocks of West Town, with trash piled to the third floor of the surrounding semicondemned redbrick tenement buildings and spilling down side streets. Dozens of people were working the mounds, dragging sacks of salvage behind them.

Mert, the woman who owned Peary Pawn and Title, had told Vick the dump started when the city ran out of money and couldn't afford to send garbage trucks around to pick up people's trash anymore. At first everyone tossed their trash out windows onto the sidewalk; then they realized it was no fun to smell their trash all day, so they started dumping it in spots where there weren't many people around to complain.

Tara was nowhere in sight. Huffing, Vick trudged

around the base of the mound he was working on, arms spread to aid his balance as his feet sank into the trash.

She was sitting on a filthy mattress on the opposite side of the mound, waving off the flies and laughing as she watched a TV show on a decrepit handheld with a missing back panel. Vick had no clue how she'd gotten it working, but it didn't surprise him. Wild audience laughter drifted from the handheld. Vick guessed she was watching *Boffo,* a reality show where people gave domestic robots tricky orders so the robots would do the wrong things and look stupid. It was one of her favorite shows.

"Tara."

She didn't hear him. Classic Tara.

He raised his voice. *"Tara."*

Her smile vanished. She went to hide the handheld behind her back, then realized it was pointless.

"Remember what those first weeks were like? Remember being really, really hungry?"

"Of course I remember." She reached up and twirled her hair nervously, glaring into empty space to Vick's right. She almost never looked to his left, always his right. And she never, ever, looked directly at him.

"If we don't work, there's no dinner."

"I *know* that. Do you think I don't know that? I know that."

"Then put the handheld away and help me." Vick held up the component he'd unearthed. "Is this any good?"

Tara rose and trudged toward him, her pet robot hopping along at her heels looking like a cross between a big rat and a rag doll, its cobbled-together parts all mismatched, its face nothing but a snout and eyes on scuffed silver metal. "Let me see."

Vick handed her the L-shaped tube. She held it close and squinted, her whole face scrunching. "It's from a dishwasher."

"Is it any good?"

Tara reared back and threw it. She didn't have much of an arm—it clattered to the ground a dozen feet away. "Sure. If you're repairing a dishwasher."

"Fine. Now can you please get back to work? This is serious. If we work hard enough, soon we'll be able to rent our own place."

"With royal blue carpet and shell tile in the kitchen. And a white concrete birdbath in the backyard in the corner by the water recycler."

A sudden wave of homesickness mixed with sympathy for Tara nearly doubled Vick over. He squeezed his eyes shut until it passed. As much as it ever passed. Routine and sameness were so important for Tara—a classic symptom of autism. "It won't be exactly the same as home, Tara. But it'll be nice. You can have your own room."

Tara just stood there, arms dangling at her sides, gazing off to Vick's right. A cloud of flies buzzed around her head. A few landed on the corners of her mouth.

"Please help me. Dig. You're the one who knows what we're looking for. What we can sell."

"Okay. I'm sorry." She knelt where she was and picked at the trash, moving it a piece at a time. The little robot sat beside her, wagging its rat tail.

"I know it's disgusting. I hate it, too."

"You can go away now. You're bothering me," Tara said.

Vick sighed as he turned away. You never had to guess with Tara; she always gave it to you straight. He headed back to his spot. Behind him Tara began humming tunelessly.

Sometimes Tara drove him crazy. Before, Mom had handled Tara's meltdowns, her insistence that *nothing* ever change—not even the order of the utensils set beside her plate. So much had changed since those days, and that meant Tara's symptoms—the meltdowns, the retreating into her own world—had gotten worse. Now they didn't *have* utensils. Sometimes they didn't even have food, although not as often as during the first awful weeks after Mom died.

Vick didn't want to think about that time. Better to think about the future. Things were looking up—they were earning a little money, and every day that went by they got a little older, a little better able to take care of themselves. Eight more months and they'd be fourteen. In a few years, thanks to Tara's brilliance with electronics, they could open their own repair shop. It felt good to have a plan, to know things were going to keep improving from here on out.

Vick stopped digging and listened. Tara had stopped working again. Sighing in frustration, he went around the mound and found her on her knees, monkeying with something she was holding close to her face.

Vick rolled his eyes toward the cloudless sky. "Please. Please stop goofing off and dig."

"I found something," Tara said, breathless.

Vick took a step toward her and tried to make out what she was holding. It was tiny, not much bigger than the flies. "Is it good? Can we use it?"

"It's . . . weird." She went on fiddling with it.

"Don't waste too much time on it," he pleaded. "You can figure out what it is tonight."

Tara didn't hear him, or pretended not to. From his angle, her profile was hidden by her dirty-blond hair (with the emphasis on *dirty*). Every morning he tied it back with a rubber band to try to keep it clean, and within an hour she took it out. She was so small she could pass for a seven-year-old. With the difference in their sizes, and Vick's dark hair and Tara's light, no one could believe they were twins.

"Come on, Tara. *Please.*"

"Okay, *fine.*" She stashed the thing in the back pocket of her jeans. Vick returned to his spot. As he dug, he pictured Tara fishing that stupid component out of her pocket as soon as he wasn't looking, and he knew—absolutely, positively knew—that was what she'd done.

"Put it away," he called, knowing she would dutifully put it away, dig for five minutes, and then take it out again. Why did he waste his breath?

CHAPTER 2

It always felt strange to step back onto pavement after sixteen hours wading on thirty feet of trash. The ground felt so hard, his feet so light.

It was almost dark, and the last sun rays gave the unlit lights down West Huron Street a glow, a reminder of when Vick was a little kid, before the economy crashed and everything turned bad. Bad in the poor neighborhoods, anyway. The lights were still shining in the wealthy neighborhoods on the north side.

After turning on North Trumbull and walking part of the way down the block, he realized Tara was no longer beside him. He jolted to a stop.

Tara was still walking straight on West Huron, staring down at the doohickey she'd found.

"Tara." His voice turned into an odd croak halfway through. Maybe his voice was changing. That would be good—if his voice got deeper and he looked more like a man, he'd come across as less of an easy target. Thirteen was a bad age to be homeless. Not young and cute enough for pity, but not old enough to hold their ground against grown-ups.

Tara stopped and looked around until she spotted Vick. She broke into a grin. "You trying to give me the slip?"

"I think it's the other way around. Come on."

She trotted to catch up, her squirrel-sized robot following dutifully. Tara's eyes suddenly grew wide, and she pointed. "*Look, look, look. It's beautiful.*" She kept on running right past Vick, her long, smooth strides eating up ground, robo-pup racing after her.

"Wait, where are you—" Then Vick spotted what had Tara so excited. Across the street, a huge watchdog was prowling along the sidewalk, accompanied by a half-dozen mean-looking guys in matching neon-green stretch shirts, their hair dyed white. The watchdog was chest-high on the men and made from gleaming chrome. Tara was heading right for it.

"Tara. *Wait.*" Vick sprinted after her, but even though

he was six inches taller and had lost those extra pounds, his twin was still faster.

A couple of the men jolted in surprise as Tara ran right up to the watchdog, chattering.

"I'm sorry. She doesn't know what she's doing," Vick said, breathless as he caught up.

"*I* don't know what I'm doing? *You* don't know what *you're* doing," Tara said.

"Don't worry about it," one of the men said, his voice a low growl. He had a bald stripe shaved down the center of his long white hair, and arms like steel pipes. "You like watchdogs?"

"I *love* watchdogs." Tara reached up and set her hand between the thing's shoulder blades, which rose and fell like levers as it walked. It didn't seem to notice. People called them watchdogs, but you could build them to look like anything—a tiger, a spider, a velociraptor—or they could resemble nothing at all. This one looked like a cross between a pit bull and a four-legged T. rex. It had an oversized head, with dozens of silver fangs bristling inside massive jaws. The body was squat and powerful, the hind legs shorter than the front ones.

One look at it was enough to know it was designed to be a fighter. It was technically illegal to create a robot designed to kill, but it was a gray area. Even a domestic robot could crush someone's windpipe, and it was hard to know what a robot could do just by looking at it. As long as you didn't outfit one with an automatic weapon you could probably get away with anything, especially in bad areas like this one. Police rarely ventured into this neighborhood anymore, and when they did they definitely had no interest in tangling with a watchdog.

"His rear hip joints are ball and socket, aren't they?" Tara asked, her blue eyes bright with interest.

"Tiny's? I have no idea," the guy said. "Somebody else designed him. I just bought him."

"For ninety grand," the tall, lean guy walking next to him muttered. "We could've bought a whole gun store for that."

The guy with the bald stripe glared. "You want to scare someone? Point a gun at him. You want him to crap his pants? Sic one of these on him."

Vick wanted to yank Tara out of there, but Stripe had said she was fine, and Vick didn't want to make Stripe angry.

"What's in the sack?" the guy trailing the pack asked Vick.

"Just . . . clothes." Vick's heart was thumping so hard he was afraid it was going to burst through his chest. "Tara, it's time to go."

Tara ignored him. She pointed at her little robo-pup, which wasn't a whole lot bigger than one of Tiny's paws clanking along the sidewalk. "I designed *my* watchdog all by myself."

The men burst out laughing.

Stripe motioned at them to cut it out, then turned back to Tara. "You really built that yourself? I'm impressed."

"I'm good with electronics."

"You must be." Stripe slowed to a halt. "Listen, we have some work to do in here, so you need to go home now, okay?"

"We don't have a home," Tara said as Vick grasped her upper arm. "We live on a roof."

Stripe gave her an impatient look. "Then go on back to your roof."

She tugged against Vick's grip as he pulled her across the street. "Ow. Let me go."

"Shut up. Come *on*."

Vick glanced back at the men, who were gathered around the watchdog. Stripe was pointing at the building's front door. "Sic 'em, Tiny. Everyone inside."

"Oh, *crud*," Vick hissed under his breath, trying not to panic. "We have to get out of here."

The watchdog lowered its massive head, opened its steel jaws, and let out a high-pitched, piercing metallic shriek.

It charged the door.

Vick wanted to run, but Tara was like an anchor.

The steel beast moved quickly, smoothly. The door snapped right in half when the watchdog hit it with his huge head, one half bursting into the street, the other buckling inward.

Shouts erupted inside.

Tara clapped her hands over her ears and squeezed her eyes closed. "I don't like that. Make it stop."

Vick tugged her down the street. He needed to get her out of earshot of those screams before she had a total meltdown. Tara stumbled along, making a panicked keening sound that grew louder and louder.

"Deep breaths, Tara." It was something Mom used to say when Tara was losing it, although, come to think of it, it had never helped much.

It didn't help now. Vick managed to get Tara a block away from the gang before she had a full-fledged meltdown right on the sidewalk, her arms and legs flailing, her screams ear-piercing. There wasn't much Vick could do except put Tara's head in his lap so she didn't bump it, and wait for her to calm down.

"It's okay. Everything's okay," he said in a soothing tone. When Mom was still alive, Tara would have maybe one of these meltdowns a month; now it was more like twice a week.

After a few minutes she stopped shrieking, rolled

onto her side, and stared at the little patch of weeds by her head.

"You okay? Ready to go home?" Vick asked.

"Okay."

Vick helped her up and brushed off her clothes.

CHAPTER 3

They stood on the rickety fire escape three stories above the city and stared at the ladder that led to the roof.

"You want to go first this time?" Tara asked.

Vick grasped the rung and stepped onto the ladder. He hated climbing this ladder, especially in the dark, and *most* especially while lugging a sack of electronic salvage. They could have taken the stairs inside, but the building was abandoned, and after sundown the stairwell was pitch-dark. Sometimes other people slept in abandoned buildings, too, and Vick liked running into them even less than he liked the fire escape. He half closed his eyes and climbed, his fingers squeezing the rusted iron so hard it hurt.

When he reached the last rung, the ladder rattled in the wind like it could pull loose from the wall at any moment. He swung the sack onto the roof, then slid on his belly over the low wall. He dropped onto the roof and turned to help Tara.

"I'm okay. I don't need any help," she protested as he pulled on her armpits. "Watch Daisy."

Daisy's little metal head was sticking out of Tara's backpack. "I thought you named it Tangelo?"

"I changed my mind." Tara stood and brushed herself off. "And she's a she, not an it."

The sight of their "home" filled Vick with relief, even though it wasn't much of a home. It was nothing but a lean-to constructed from salvaged plywood, cardboard, and plastic trash bags. They couldn't even stand up inside. Parts were strewn across the roof, including three big piles by the far wall. Because it came from the dump, the debris gave off a sour stink.

There was the faintest nip of coolness in the late-August air. Another two months and it would be too cold to sleep there; they'd have to go back to sleeping at the Salvation Army shelter. Vick dreaded going back there. It was packed with people, a lot of them scary-looking, and anything you didn't carry around all the time got stolen. Besides, Vick preferred it when they were on their own. Once upon a time he'd trusted adults to watch out for him. Not anymore.

Vick unloaded the day's haul of electronic salvage from the sack, separating it into robot parts they could clean up and sell to dealers at the flea market, and phone/TV/computer stuff they'd try to sell to the pawnshop, if Tara could fix them.

When he was finished, he crawled inside the lean-to and opened the Styrofoam cooler that served as their kitchen. He took out the food that was left in it: half a can of corned beef hash, a sleeve of saltines, the last three Chips Ahoy! chocolate chip cookies in an otherwise empty package.

He scooted out of the lean-to, holding two plates. "Dinner's ready."

Tara was hunched over Daisy, simultaneously working on her and whispering to her. She accepted the food without looking Vick's way. Usually this was when she'd launch into a tirade about what they were *supposed* to be having for dinner (chicken quesadillas with American cheese and bacon crumbles—don't cook them too long because they're not good when the edges are crunchy—corn on the cob with butter not margarine, potato puffs, 2 percent chocolate milk), but she just went on monkeying with Daisy.

"If you're going to work, could you work on fixing some of the stuff we brought back?"

Tara ignored him.

"Fine." Vick went to the edge of the roof and watched vehicles and people pass below while he ate his pathetic dinner.

This was the hardest part of the day for him. The dump was awful, but usually he was too busy and miserable to feel scared. It was here, on this big, dark, empty roof, when he felt most strongly how alone they were. It felt like a block of ice in his gut.

His entire life seemed like a slow-motion fall down a flight of stairs. First his father lost their house trying to start a business and ran away in shame. Then Mom lost her job at Versacci's Beauty Spa to a robot that worked for free and never needed a lunch break, and she had to take the job installing solar panels, because it was one of the few jobs robots couldn't do that you could get without a college degree. Then the freak accident where the solar panel broke loose and fell, and Uncle Mason and Aunt Ruby saying they couldn't afford to take care of Tara and him even though they were supposed to be their godparents.

Vick had been an honors student, back when his mother was alive. Now he'd missed sixth grade. Every day he wasn't in school, he fell farther behind. Every day he grew a little dumber compared to the kids who were going to school.

One of the knee-high cleanup bots Tara had built from junk parts tottered past him on its stubby legs. It was wearing a soiled pink party dress Tara had salvaged from the dump that must have come from some kid's doll, plus a partially crushed red felt hat with a white bow that looked ridiculous on its square aluminum head. The other bot was dressed as a boy. They were supposed to be Chloe and Jack—the brother and sister from Technopunks, Tara's favorite book series.

"Chloe looks bored," Vick said. He spotted Jack on the other end of the roof, wandering aimlessly. "So does Jack."

Tara went on tinkering, her lips moving soundlessly.

Vick watched Chloe scan the ground for small pieces of junk she could put away. That's all they did, day and night. You had to be careful what you set down, because Chloe and Jack couldn't tell the difference between trash and valuables. It all went in the trash bin.

"Hey, Chloe?"

Chloe, whose voice recognition software had registered her name, stopped walking and waited for Vick to give her further instructions.

"Move all of the parts in the green bin into the red bin." That ought to keep her busy for a while.

The little bot headed straight for the green bin, which was filled with gutted parts from unfixable electronic devices. Vick knew Chloe was just a bunch of wires and circuits and programs, but he couldn't help thinking she looked happy to have something to do as she scooped an armful of parts from the green bin.

"That's great. Thanks, Chloe." Of course, she'd be finished in ten minutes and would have nothing to do again.

Vick eyed Jack, who was now near the steel door that led into the inner stairwell. He suppressed a laugh. "Jack? Move all the parts in the red bin to the green bin."

Jack took off toward the red bin.

"Thanks, buddy."

Chloe dropped a handful of parts into the red bin, then hurried back to the green bin to get more. Jack bent, scooped up an armful of parts from the red bin, and headed toward the green bin.

Vick burst out laughing. "Good job, guys. You're doing great."

Tara looked up from her work. "What are you doing?" She watched the bots.

Chloe and Jack passed each other, each carrying parts. Vick laughed harder. The longer they did it, the funnier it got.

"You goofball!" Tara said.

"They were *bored*," Vick managed, then broke down laughing again as Jack and Chloe dropped their parts and marched past each other toward opposite bins to get more.

Tara started laughing. "*Aw.* The poor knuckle-heads don't know any better." She watched the two bots and laughed harder. Vick was laughing so hard, tears streamed down his cheeks.

A shout from below jolted Vick.

They stopped laughing. Tara hurried over to see who it was as Vick turned to look down at the street.

Two guys came running around the corner carrying boxes. He'd seen them on the street before, milling around outside gambling stores and pool halls. One was white with long dreadlocks, the other black with a shaved head. Both were a little older than Vick. They stopped out of sight, directly below Vick.

"Did they see you?" one of the guys said.

"I don't know. Nobody looked right *at* me, I don't think."

"I want to go home!" Tara cried out. Vick nearly jumped out of his skin in surprise. He sprang at Tara, shushing violently.

"Right now!" Tara wailed.

Vick clamped his hand over her mouth.

He could hear the voices trail up from the street. "What was that?" one of the guys asked.

Tara struggled and tried to shriek right through his hand. Vick pressed tighter.

"I don't know," the other guy said. Then, much louder: "Who's up there?"

Vick dragged Tara back toward their lean-to.

"Come on down, or I'm coming up after you." Something clanged against the fire escape, hard. "Don't make me come up there."

They reached the door of the lean-to. Vick squatted and pulled Tara into the darkness.

"We have to hide," he said, his mouth close to her ear. "And you have to be quiet. You *have* to." Vick went to the back corner and slid aside the panel that led to their hiding place. "You first. Go." He urged Tara toward the narrow opening. She wriggled through. Vick followed as the clanging continued. He slid the panel back in place and huddled beside Tara in the narrow space between the back of their lean-to and the concrete wall of the stairwell.

"I'm coming to get you." Both guys laughed. Vick was beginning to suspect the boys were only trying to scare them, because they were still on the street, but you could never tell for sure who was just a jerk, and who was truly dangerous.

Tara pressed against him. "I want to go back to our nice warm home."

"Shh. *Whisper.*"

"I want Mom to come and get us," Tara whispered.

"You know she's not."

Tara nodded against his shoulder. "I know."

"But everything's going to be okay anyway," Vick said.

"How is everything going to be okay?" Tara sounded annoyed.

Vick shushed her again, because her voice was rising. It had gone quiet outside, but he didn't want to take any chances. Maybe they were coming up the fire escape.

"Who's going to make it okay?" Tara asked, whispering again.

"We are. You and me."

Tara was quiet, evidently mulling this over.

Vick waited a half hour before climbing out and scanning the streets. The guys were nowhere in sight.

When Vick returned to the lean-to, Tara was working on her puppy-bot by the light of their flashlight, a cable running from Daisy to her salvaged laptop. To preserve the battery, they were only supposed to use the flashlight in emergencies, but Vick was too tired to argue.

Vick curled up in the pile of laundry that was his bed and studied the things he'd taken with him when they were kicked out of their apartment eight months ago: a stack of comics, his baseball glove, his video games and portable player, a photo album, Mom's judo black belt, his inhaler. That was all he had in the world, besides the junk outside. They'd only been able to take what they could carry, and mostly that was stuff Tara insisted she couldn't live without. Things like her plastic toy robot collection and the Disney Purple Girls shirt that hadn't fit since she was four. He'd been stupid to let her load them up with so much junk when they could have been carrying food and medicine, but he'd been so sure this was temporary, that some adult was going to swoop in to save them. He hadn't realized that when things got bad, when there weren't enough jobs and people were hungry, adults only took care of their own kids. Some people could look so kind; then when Vick asked for help their eyes would get hard and they'd look right through him.

Vick picked up his inhaler and weighed it in his palm, trying to divine how many pumps it had left. He'd had more asthma attacks than usual since Mom died, which wasn't surprising considering what they'd been through. He'd only used the inhaler twice, when it got really bad. Once the inhaler was empty, he was in trouble.

He was almost asleep when he realized Tara still had the flashlight on. "Don't stay up too late," he muttered.

She didn't answer.

CHAPTER 4

For the first couple of seconds after Vick woke, he thought he was back in his bedroom. Then his eyes focused on the warped, splintered plywood two feet above his head, and he remembered, and the knot in his stomach returned.

When he sat up he saw Tara wasn't in the lean-to. He crawled outside into the dim light of dawn.

Tara was kneeling beside Daisy, who had her little metal face all but buried in the guts of an old Python phone. It looked like she was chewing on it.

"Please tell me you weren't up all night playing with your robot." Tara looked bleary-eyed but wired. She could get so excited about something that she shut everything else out. Vick stepped closer and squinted. "What's she doing with that phone? Take it away from her—"

Vick froze. Daisy wasn't chewing on it; she was moving her little paws around on it. Almost like she was working on it.

"What is she doing?"

Tara laughed with delight. "Trying to fix it."

Daisy set the Python phone down, then moved to a second, partly crushed phone sitting nearby. She extracted some tiny part with her teeth.

"How did you get her to do that?"

"I'm a supergenius. That's how." Tara giggled.

Tara's toy was trying to repair a phone. Vick looked from Daisy to Tara and back again. "Is she doing the right things? I mean, is it really fixing it, or just moving stuff around?"

Tara's grin widened. "She's doing fine. Aren't you, Daisy?"

Daisy looked at Tara and nodded.

This was a toy. It was supposed to understand basic commands like *come* and *stay*. You had to pay thousands and thousands of dollars for a robot that understood sentences and answered you.

What did a robot that could repair phones cost?

There was no such thing as a robot that could repair phones on its own.

"Can you make more of those?" Vick pointed at Daisy.

"Nope."

"Why not?"

"I don't have the right part."

Vick tried not to let his disappointment show. "What part?"

"The one that makes her smart."

Vick nodded. "Why don't we head to the dump and see if we can find what you need?" If Tara could make more of them, they could make a lot of money. A *lot* of money.

Vick washed up using the rainwater they had collected by diverting it from the gutters, then changed into one of the cleanish shirts he'd washed in the same water and draped on a railing to dry.

As they headed for the dump, Daisy didn't follow at Tara's heels like she usually did. She was all over the place, sometimes running ahead, sometimes disappearing from sight before reappearing from a completely different direction.

"What's she doing?" Vick finally asked when Daisy disappeared yet again.

Tara shrugged. "I don't know."

"You didn't give her a command?"

"Nope." Tara giggled and clapped her hands together. "You should see the look on your face."

Vick scanned the streets for the little robot, but it was nowhere in sight. A flicker of motion from above caught his attention: it was Daisy, airborne, leaping from one roof to the next. "Holy—" What was she *doing*?

Vick caught a whiff of the dump. They were still three blocks away, but the smell carried.

Up ahead, Daisy turned a corner and raced toward them. As she drew close, she started making a strange *bloop* sound, her hindquarters bouncing into the air.

"What is she doing now?" Vick asked.

"No idea. She's blooping."

They passed her. She got in front of them again and blooped.

"Settle down, girl," Tara said. Immediately, Daisy fell into step beside Tara. They approached the dump for another stinking day of trash-digging.

As they climbed the edge of the pile, Vick could see something was wrong. None of the usual pickers were in the dump. Instead, people in gas masks and plastic clothes were spread evenly across the mounds.

"Hey." A guy in a gas mask headed toward them across the trash. "The dump is closed."

"How can it be closed? Nobody owns it." There wasn't another dump in walking distance. Without this place, they wouldn't eat.

The guy lifted his gas mask, and Vick immediately recognized him. Stripe. "You two again. I've got a long day ahead of me and I'm in a crappy mood, so don't argue, just get lost."

"Well, you can't tell us where we can walk," Tara shot back.

Stripe stuck his fingers in his mouth and whistled.

In answer to his whistle, Stripe's watchdog, Tiny, cleared a rise, racing toward them. Stripe gave Vick a steely glare. "I said it's closed, man. Take your dimwit sister and get lost."

Tara surged forward, her face reddening. "Don't call me a dimwit. I'll bet I'm smarter than you are, pinhead."

Vick grabbed Tara's shoulders and turned her around, expecting Stripe to sic the watchdog on them at any second. He could still hear that awful screeching sound it had made before it crashed through that apartment door.

"Hang on," Stripe said.

Reluctantly, Vick turned back.

Stripe was staring at Daisy, who was right at Tara's heels, looking up at them. "You said you designed that?"

"That's right."

Stripe squatted beside Daisy. "How'd you design those hip joints?"

Tara frowned, trying to find the words. "It's not ball and socket. More like a K-joint, but two K-joints on top of each other." She gave Stripe a satisfied grin. "Now who's a dimwit?"

Stripe curled his finger at Daisy. "Let me see her."

"*No!*" Tara shouted.

"Just for a minute." Stripe stepped toward her.

"No. Daisy, *run*." As soon as the words left Tara's lips, Daisy took off.

Stripe pointed at the fleeing figure. "Tiny, fetch."

Tiny took off after Daisy.

Daisy didn't make it a hundred yards. The gleaming chrome monster pinned her with a front paw, snapped her up in his jaws, and brought her back to Stripe.

Stripe turned Daisy over, grasped one of her rear legs, and moved it back and forth.

"Leave her alone." Tara lunged, but Vick held her back.

Stripe raised Daisy out of Tara's reach. "I'm gonna hang on to this for a while. Now get out of here."

Tara went nuts. She tore loose from Vick and launched herself at Stripe, trying to pry Daisy from his grip. When she didn't come loose, Tara bit Stripe's arm.

"No!" Vick leaped to protect Tara as Stripe knocked her to the ground.

"Get *off* me." Stripe examined his forearm. "Dang. You're pushing me, kid." It was red, with clearly visible tooth marks, but it wasn't bleeding. He flipped Daisy over. "Here, you want her back?" He grasped one of Daisy's hind legs and tore it off, his big bicep bulging like it was going to push right through the skin. He tossed the rest of Daisy to the ground beside Tara. "All I need is this joint. Now get lost, and don't let me catch you back here."

Howling, Tara swept Daisy up and hugged her to her chest.

Vick drew Tara to her feet. "We have to go, Tara. Right now."

"Look what he did! Look what he did to Daisy. *Bully!*" Tara looked devastated.

"You can fix her good as new. Come on. Quick. Quick." Vick got her moving.

When they were out of the dump, Tara set Daisy down. "Can you walk, girl?"

At first Daisy tried to walk as if the leg was still there, and stumbled badly. Then she adjusted, hopping along on one back leg as if she'd been doing it the whole time.

"What are we going to do without our dump?" Vick

asked. He couldn't stand the thought of going back to standing in endless lines at churches and government ration stations, trying to get handouts before they ran out, wolfing them down before someone bigger snatched them away. Why were those people suddenly interested in the dump? The salvage in it wasn't worth much. Vick should know.

Wait. Surely they wouldn't be there at night. He and Tara could go after dark with the flashlight. They'd have to stick close together, since they only had the one flashlight, and they'd have to spend a lot more on batteries, but it was better than nothing. With any luck they'd find the part Tara needed to make more Daisys. Then they'd have enough to buy a bunch of batteries. A bunch of food, too.

"Danger," Tara said.

"What?"

"The blooping sound. Daisy was trying to warn us there was danger ahead."

No robot should be able to figure out whether something was dangerous or not, but Daisy *had* kept getting in front of them, like she wanted them to stop. "Maybe you're right."

"Of course I'm right," Tara said.

"What else can she do?"

"I don't know."

Vick stopped walking. "You *built* her. How can you not know?"

Tara gave him an impatient huff. "I built her out of used parts. Even her brain. I didn't program the chips; I just installed them and added a few things."

That made sense. Tara was a tech genius, but when would she have had time to program something as sophisticated as Daisy clearly was? "What kind of things did you add?"

"That she should never hurt anyone, and she's loyal only to me and you. The rest of what's in there was too complicated. I couldn't understand most of it."

When they had time, Vick needed to figure out exactly what the little bot could do.

CHAPTER 5

It was too dark to see Daisy, but occasionally Vick heard her steel feet scrabbling on the concrete nearby. As they got close to the dump, Daisy showed up in front of them and made the blooping sound again.

Tara stopped walking. "Danger."

Vick closed his eyes for a second, frustrated. They had to work. They *had* to. "Let's get close enough to see. If anyone's there, we'll leave."

Tara clearly didn't like that plan, but she followed along as Vick approached the dump. He pressed close to the buildings so it would be harder for someone to spot him from the dump, if anyone was there at this hour.

In the light of a half-moon hanging in the sky above the tenements, the dump was silent. Even the flies were asleep. That was a bonus to working nights that hadn't even occurred to Vick.

"Let's go." Vick climbed into the trash. The darkness did nothing to lessen the stench, unfortunately.

When he crested the mound, he saw the dump was now divided with ropes into square sections, like an archaeological site. Weird. He picked a section at random, stepped over the rope, and handed the flashlight to Tara. "Why don't you hold the flashlight while I dig?"

Tara turned on the flashlight and aimed it at the ground. Vick got to work, wondering what was going on here. What was the point of roping the dump off like that?

"What sort of parts are we looking for, to make more robots like Daisy?" Vick's words were partially drowned out by Daisy, who'd started blooping again. Vick surveyed the dump, but it was silent and empty.

Oh, no. No it wasn't. Vick's legs felt like they were turning to liquid. Tiny was racing across the dump toward them, his enormous T. rex head bobbing.

"Run."

Tara took off, and Vick followed. As they raced down the hill, Tara lost her footing and tumbled forward. She stuck out her hands to break her fall, landed halfway down the hill, and slid, an avalanche of garbage cascading along with her.

Vick rushed after her and helped her up.

The watchdog stepped out in front of them, making a low, rolling, mechanical growl. Its knees were bent, ready to leap.

Vick froze. "Stand still."

Tara buried her face in Vick's shoulder. "I don't like this. I don't like that noise."

Vick grasped Tara's shoulders. "You *have* to stay calm. We need to stay still and not upset it."

"I can't help it. You know I can't help it," Tara said. She was trembling all over.

"You *have* to, Tara. Think of a way. You're smart—you can figure this out." Vick didn't know enough about watchdogs to know what might provoke it to attack. It looked ready to spring, that terrible growl going on and on, its beady black eyes locked on them. Watchdogs were built in people's garages and basements, so each was unique and had unique programming. Back in his past life Vick had thought they were so cool; he had read all about them on the Internet. He didn't think they were cool now.

"Maybe I can put it off until later," Tara said.

"Good idea. As soon as we're home, you can let it out."

"Okay. I'll try."

While Tara struggled to hold off her meltdown, Vick tried backing them up. The pitch of the watchdog's growl grew higher and it took a warning step forward.

Daisy was about a dozen feet behind the watchdog, pacing, like she was trying to figure out what to do. What *could* she do? The thing would bite her in half if she got near it.

"We're okay." Vick squeezed Tara's arm. "We'll just stay right here. That man will come and call it off."

"He's a turd. He hurt Daisy."

Vick couldn't argue with that, even if Tara had replaced Daisy's leg in no time at all. What would he do if he found them back here again? Probably sic his watchdog on them. Vick tried to think of something to do, but there was nothing. If he still owned a phone that worked, he could try calling for help. Surely the police came if you flat-out called them. Unless someone wandered by and he could get them to call 911, though, he was out of luck.

All they could do was sit in the trash and hope Stripe would set them free with another warning.

"Daisy, go home," Tara called. "Wait there."

Daisy ran off. No use risking Stripe tearing off another limb, or maybe her head this time.

As they settled into the trash, Tara pressed close to

Vick. Mom had told him most kids with autism didn't like to be touched or held. Not Tara. When she was scared she went overboard the other way, pretty much climbing into your lap and squeezing you until you couldn't breathe.

...

A vehicle engine woke Vick. He wasn't surprised Tara had fallen asleep after staying up all night the night before, but he couldn't believe he'd managed to sleep with that massive, lantern-jawed, razor-toothed watchdog standing two steps away.

The van door slammed. Stripe was carrying a cup of coffee. He didn't seem surprised to see them; in fact, he seemed almost happy.

"Unbelievable." He patted the watchdog's massive head before pulling out his phone and making a call. "Remember the hip-socket designer? Yeah. She's right here." After a few minutes' conversation Stripe put away the phone and smiled at Vick and Tara. "I set aside the whole morning to find you, and here you are. Now I don't know what I'm going to do with myself. Maybe I'll go to the movies."

"Why did you want to find us?" Vick didn't know

whether to be relieved or scared. Stripe was taking their trespass much better than Vick had expected.

Stripe took a swig of coffee, then wiped his mouth with the back of his hand. "The boss wants to talk to you. Well, to her, actually." He gestured at Tara. "Be polite. Call her Ms. Alba or ma'am."

The boss wanted to talk to Tara about Daisy's hip design. That didn't sound so bad. Tara could tell Ms. Alba or ma'am everything she wanted to know, and then they could go home. They'd still have the problem of what they were going to eat today, but at least they'd be free from Tiny and these people.

Before long a black Maserati Air pulled up to the edge of the dump, and an Asian woman stepped out. She was dressed in white leather, with a flowing red robe that nearly reached the filthy ground. She looked like a rock star, and strutted like one as she stopped just short of the trash, glanced at Tiny, and said, "Off. Go."

The watchdog trotted away.

"Which of you is my hip designer?" The woman folded her arms and studied Vick, then Tara. Vick had never felt so filthy and smelly as he did in the presence of this clean, brilliantly dressed woman.

Tara raised her hand. "I am. I'm the hip designer."

"Come here."

Vick followed Tara down the hill of trash as Ms. Alba stepped closer. "What's your name, honey?"

"Tara."

"Tara, ma'am," Stripe corrected her, his arms folded across his chest.

Tara looked at Stripe, her eyebrows pinched in confusion.

"Well, Tara, how would you like to work for me?" Ms. Alba asked.

It took a moment for the words to sink in. Work? A paycheck? They could get an apartment, eat three meals a day. "You'd have to hire me, too."

Ms. Alba gave Vick an annoyed look. "And why is that?"

"I'm her assistant, and her twin brother. She has to stay close to me. She has autism."

"That's true. I'm severely autistic," Tara chimed in. "But I don't mind—it's probably the reason I can design hip joints so well."

"Fine, you can both work." Ms. Alba turned to Stripe. "Pack them up. I'll meet you at the shop."

"Let's go." Stripe gestured toward the open hatch of his beat-up white van. There were no seats. They sat on the floor beside a stack of cardboard boxes.

"Any luck?" Ms. Alba asked Stripe as they waited. She was looking up at the dump.

"Not yet, but we'll find it," Stripe said.

Ms. Alba kicked an aluminum can lying beside her foot. Her glistening high-heeled boots looked like they were made of polished silver. "Those idiots." She headed to her sports car without a glance back.

"Tiny. Up." Stripe slapped the rear bumper of the van. The watchdog climbed in; the back of the van sank under his weight. Vick and Tara scurried deeper into the van until they were pressed against the wall that separated the back of the van from the seats.

Clinging to the sides to keep from sliding when the van turned, they eyed the watchdog as it lay in front of the door, its massive head raised, beady black eyes staring back at them.

"I don't like this. At all," Tara said, glancing around.

Vick swallowed and tried to fight off a growing sense that he'd made a mistake. "It's okay. We work for them now. They won't hurt us, and we can save up some money." Except they made watchdogs that hurt people. He'd temporarily forgotten that—he'd been too busy thinking about the money they'd make.

CHAPTER 6

When the rear doors swung open, they were in the parking lot of a body shop strewn with rusted-out vehicle parts and cars with flat tires, or no tires at all, lined up against a chain-link fence topped with barbed wire.

Just as Vick turned away, he caught a glimpse of movement on the roof of the doughnut shop beyond that fence. He turned back and studied the spot, but there was nothing there.

"This way." Stripe pointed toward an open roll-up door.

"You know, on second thought, I don't think we're

old enough to be working here," Vick said. "Maybe we'll just go home."

Stripe shook his head. "Sorry, kid, you'll have to discuss that with Ms. Alba, and I don't think she'll be happy about you going back on your word."

Vick stayed beside the van, with Tara pressed close to him. "Believe me, Tara would be the worst employee you've ever had."

Tara nodded in agreement. "Plus it's against the law. You have to be sixteen to work."

Stripe laughed at that. "Don't worry, we have special permission from the mayor. There are lots of kids your age and younger working for us. Now come on, let's go."

Vick's heart was tripping wildly as Stripe led them through the body shop to a back staircase, down to a huge, low-ceilinged basement. Thirty or more people were working under bright lights, bent over parts, operating machines, working blowtorches. They were building watchdogs. Most were kids, although one man was at least eighty.

Ms. Alba was waiting on the shop floor. She led them across the grease-stained concrete to a dim office that stank of cigarettes. A big woman with dyed red hair was working at a computer while smoking.

"Dixie, I've got a couple of new workers for you."

Ms. Alba put her hand on Tara's head. "This one is a whiz. Put her in R and D."

Dixie grunted. "What's wrong with her? She looks weird."

Vick braced himself for Tara's outrage at being called weird, but she only stood there, arms dangling loosely, her whole body trembling.

"She has autism." Vick's voice sounded shaky and timid to his own ears.

"Yeah, whatever." Dixie's chair screeched as she stood. On her way over she plucked two black tubes from a glass jar. Ms. Alba reached down and grabbed Vick's wrist; then she grabbed Tara's with her other hand.

"What are you doing?" Vick took an instinctive step back.

"Just hold still." Dixie was chewing gum, working it furiously. She set one of the tubes down. Vick tried to pull away.

"Hold still, or it'll hurt like crazy and we'll have to do it all over again." Dixie lifted the tube and jabbed it against his arm. It felt like a huge wasp was stinging him, the stinger sinking deep and staying for a long time as Vick grunted, his jaw clamped tight against the pain.

Finally she pulled it free, and he realized it was some sort of syringe. "See? That wasn't so bad."

"What did you do? What was that?" Vick pressed

his hand over his arm. The spot was still throbbing and burning.

Dixie set down the spent syringe, and then quickly picked up the other as Tara tried to pull free from Ms. Alba.

"Hold still." She pressed it to Tara's arm as Stripe held Vick back.

Tara shrieked in fear and pain as the shot stung her arm.

When Ms. Alba and Stripe let them go, Tara threw her arms around Vick, and Vick hugged his twin sister fiercely, rocking her gently. "We're okay. It's over now. It's over."

Dixie and Ms. Alba stood over them, waiting.

"Move away from the door," Dixie said, grasping the knob. Vick moved Tara. Dixie opened the door and called, "Tiny. Come."

Vick heard Tiny's metal claws on the concrete floor before he saw him, his chrome body glistening in the light, filling the doorway.

Dixie looked down at Vick and Tara. "What we injected into you was a tracer. If you run away, Tiny will know just where you ran. He'll come after you and drag you back here. You understand?"

Over Dixie's shoulder, Vick saw a window high up on the wall. It had heavy steel bars across it. Vick wanted to tell this woman that they couldn't get away with pulling kids off the street in broad daylight. But the truth was, they could. No one would be looking for them.

Dixie curled a finger toward Tara. "Come on, I'll show you where you'll be working."

Vick leaped to his feet. "We have to stay together. She can't be on her own."

Dixie scowled at him. "She won't be on her own."

"I mean, she has to be with me or she'll lose it."

Every word Vick uttered seemed to make Dixie angrier. "You know what your sister's problem is? I'll give you a hint: it's not autism. Her problem is she's a sissy. She needs to toughen up. And now's as good a time as any to start."

Ms. Alba nodded briskly. "She'll get used to it. We need you doing other things."

As soon as Dixie bent and pulled Tara to her feet, Tara started wailing. Vick tried to follow her, but Ms. Alba held him back.

"You don't understand; she can't control it. I have to stay with her or she won't be able to work for you."

"That's enough. Let's go." Ms. Alba led Vick to the main floor, to a tall, gangly, dark-skinned girl who looked like she was Vick's age, maybe a year older. Ms. Alba told the girl to show him what to do, then headed for the exit without another word, and nothing Vick said about Tara got a second glance. When he followed her to the door, protesting, Stripe stood in his path. "Back to your station, kid."

It was agonizing to hear Tara's wails and not be able to help her. He went back to the table with the tall girl and stared at the door where they'd taken Tara.

"There's nothing you can do right now," the girl said. "You need to pretend to work, at least." Her name was East, and she said she'd been in that basement for three months. Vick had picked up enough of the basics of DIY robotics from Tara that they could talk in low voices while Vick pretended he was getting the hang of things. It was hard to concentrate with Tara wailing in another room.

"All Alba cares about is getting rich—like, private jets and bodyguards rich," East was saying as she worked on a spine. Her curly hair was pulled back away from her face with a rubber band. "She thinks watchdogs are her ticket."

"She thinks she's going to get rich enough to fly in private jets making watchdogs?"

"They aren't just some hobby thing people do in their garages anymore." East wiped sweat from her forehead with the grease-stained back of her wrist. "Gangs are buying them up, even some regular people looking to protect themselves from the gangs. A bunch of little underground shops have sprung up. That's how I got by, before I ended up here. Me and my friends jacked domestic bots and chopped them up to build watchdogs."

Vick struggled not to look surprised. This thirteen-year-old got by stealing robots and turning them into bodyguards?

"Alba's trying to drive all the little shops out of business, one way or another, and corner the market. Create a watchdog empire here in Chicago."

"Using hostages to build them," Vick said.

"Like I said, she'll do whatever it takes. Ruthless is her middle name. She pretty much owns this part of the city. The police do what she tells them; the gangs don't dare cross her. I'm surprised you haven't heard of her."

"Yeah, well, we don't get out much," Vick said. "We've been trying hard to keep to ourselves." He looked around. "Not that it did much good."

In the other room Tara cried on, her voice growing hoarse.

"You a Brumby?" East asked.

"What's a Brumby?"

East gave him a look. "Street kid. Orphan."

"Oh. Yeah. Our mom died eight months ago. How about you?"

"I've been on the street for three years. I grew up a couple of blocks from here. My folks kicked me out after

Dad lost his job. They said they couldn't afford to feed all of us, so they kicked out me and two brothers and kept my two sisters."

Vick fumbled and nearly dropped the miniature socket wrench he was using. "That's harsh. How did they decide who went and who stayed?"

East shrugged. "Just who'd been good and who hadn't." She said it matter-of-factly, but she had to look away when she said it. Vick bet it still hurt.

In the next room Dixie shouted, "You want something to cry about? You don't work, you don't eat. How do you like that?"

East must have seen him flinch. "You need to talk to your sister. If she gives them grief, they're going to make her life miserable. Yours, too."

Talk to his sister. If things had been different, he might have laughed at that. "She's autistic. When she gets like that, it's like a switch was flipped in her head. She can't help it. You might as well tell the wind not to blow." Although, she'd managed to hold it off when they were in the dump with Tiny looming over them. Maybe she was getting control of that switch.

A watchdog clinked past them, all jet-black steel except for yellow eyes, so big he probably couldn't have fit through a normal-sized door. It didn't look *that* much like a grizzly—its mouth was much bigger and wider than a grizzly's, its limbs leaner, and it had no ears—but Vick had a habit of thinking about watchdogs in terms of the animal they resembled most.

The grizzly disappeared through a double-wide doorway into the back of the shop. Vick wondered how many of them Ms. Alba had.

CHAPTER 7

Dinner was leftovers from other people's lunches—ham sandwiches that smelled off, some half-eaten, and stale bagels. Vick stuffed his half bagel into his pocket when no one was looking.

When they went to bed on the shop floor, on mattresses that looked and smelled like they'd been salvaged from the dump, he slipped the bagel to Tara. Her dirty face was lined with tear tracks, and her eyes were bloodshot.

"I want potato puffs," she whispered. "Chicken quesadillas with American cheese and bacon crumbles. Don't cook them too long. The edges shouldn't be crunchy. Corn on the cob. Butter, never margarine."

"For God's sake, be quiet," said the old man, whose name was Arthur.

Vick squeezed his eyes shut. He wasn't sure he could take this without losing his mind. He opened them and took a few deep breaths, trying to get himself under control.

Something scurried across the floor.

Vick bolted upright and yanked his feet from the edge of the mattress. A rat?

"What the matter?" Tara asked.

"Did you see that?"

"What?"

It scurried onto Vick's bed. Shrieking, he leaped out of bed, his heart hammering. He got a better look at it by the dim light bleeding from the hall.

It was Daisy.

...

"How did she find us?" Vick asked in a harsh whisper.

"I don't know."

Somehow she'd unlocked both heavy steel doors, which had combination locks. Vick and Tara were free. Except for the tracking devices, and Tiny.

"I don't care," Tara said when Vick reminded her about Tiny. "I don't care. I want to get out of here."

"Send that darned thing away and get in bed," Arthur said from his mattress. "They'll kill you. They're not fooling around."

"Shut up and mind your own business," Tara snapped at him.

East, who'd been hovering nearby, watching quietly, stepped closer. "I don't mean to interrupt, but I'm out of here. It was nice meeting you both." She headed for the door before Vick could reply.

A few others followed East's lead, but not all of them. Not even most of them. Vick wasn't sure what to do. He didn't want to stay, not another minute. But what about Tiny?

Would Tiny come after them immediately, or would they get a head start? Maybe he was locked up somewhere and wouldn't be sent after them until Dixie and Ms. Alba discovered they were gone.

Tara raised her head and looked just to Vick's right. Not a few feet to his right, more like six inches. As far as he could remember, it was the closest she'd ever come to looking him in the eye. "Please. I can't stay here. I'll die."

Daisy hopped off the bed, walked halfway to the door, and then spun around and returned.

"Okay."

"You're out of your mind," one of the kids called from the darkness on the other side of the room.

"Let them go," Arthur said. "They'll learn."

They headed for the door. Daisy followed them up the stairs, through the silent garage, and out a side door that had a ragged Daisy-sized hole in the glass.

As soon as they got outside, they ran.

"We need to find a police station," Vick said. Would the police protect them, though? East had said the police did what Ms. Alba told them to do.

Daisy darted ahead, then veered to the left. She looked back to make sure they were following. She was smart—smarter than any robot Vick had ever seen, even on TV. What sort of robot understood you were in danger and figured out how to save you? If only she were ten times bigger, they wouldn't have to worry about Tiny.

Vick stopped running. "Hang on."

Daisy stopped, too. She looked around, evidently watching for danger.

"Tara? Can you build a watchdog? Like Tiny?"

"No."

"Oh." Vick tried not to let his disappointment show. He wasn't exactly surprised by her answer, but he'd hoped—

"I mean, I *can*," Tara went on, "but I wouldn't. It's a *terrible* design. I'd do it way better." She shook her head. "Way better."

Vick burst out laughing. "Fine. Make it way better. Can you give it Daisy's brain?"

Tara looked startled. "That's a *brilliant* idea. You're a genius."

"Daisy," Vick called. "Take us to our roof. You're getting a makeover."

CHAPTER 8

Vick stood behind Tara, shifting from foot to foot, waiting. Tara opened and closed the jaws she'd fashioned from air conditioner blades and the hinge from a Ford Sol's trunk. Most of the main body was made from domestic bot parts. Suddenly the piles of seemingly useless parts they'd accumulated on the roof might save their lives, and while Vick sucked at designing and building, he rocked when it came to finding just the right part.

"What do you need?" he asked.

"Quiet."

Vick shut his mouth. It was hard, not knowing how long they had before Tiny showed up, and whether the steel bars he'd wedged across the door to the roof would keep him out.

Since Tara didn't need him, he went over to where Daisy was working diligently on what would soon be her own hind legs. They looked good—they were bowed, lean yet powerful-looking. Daisy had finished the front legs, which had sharp claws, but hands like a squirrel's instead of a dog's. Vick couldn't quite believe this little robot was helping design her own new body. Robots didn't *design*. A high-end domestic robot couldn't decide what brand of coffee to buy unless you told it exactly. It would stand in the coffee section of the supermarket for eternity, trapped in a decision-loop.

Daisy set one leg down, then picked up the other.

Vick wasn't surprised that Tara was making it look like a dog (a dog with squirrel hands and a pointed snout, but it still looked more like a dog than anything else). She'd always wanted a dog. Mom would never get one, because a lot of apartments didn't allow them, and it was hard enough finding an apartment in Chicago when you didn't have a pet.

From the looks of it, it wasn't going to have a tail. Most watchdogs didn't, because tails served no purpose on a robot. Most also had at least four legs, because that made them faster. Plus, two-legged watchdogs tended to tip over.

On the roof beyond Daisy, Jack and Chloe were still at work, moving the parts in the green bin to the red bin and vice versa.

"Chloe, that's enough. Stop," Vick called. "Jack—"

A low metallic squeal rose from behind the door that led down from the roof, filling Vick with a sick dread. It was the same noise Tiny had made when he'd trapped them at the dump. A sharp *bang* on the door made him flinch. Another followed almost immediately.

Vick took a few wobbly steps until he could see the door, which was made of thick steel, the hinges rusty but anchored into the frame on heavy steel plates.

Another *bang*. Tiny must be hitting the door from the inside. He squealed louder.

"The longer you make me stand here, the angrier I'm going to get," Dixie yelled. The doorknob jiggled. "Unlock this door. Right now."

Vick turned to Tara, who was working to attach the jaws to the rest of the head while whispering to herself. "Tara, just make it good enough. You can make it perfect later."

Tara didn't answer. She was so absorbed in what she was doing it was possible she hadn't even heard Tiny or Vick. He studied the scattered pieces of their to-be watchdog, trying to guess how close they were to finishing. He had no idea. Maybe less than an hour, maybe six.

He jogged over to a gutted refrigerator lying on its side, got behind it, and pushed, rolling it over. He kept rolling it until it was pressed against the door.

"Get 'em. Go get 'em," Dixie urged from behind the door.

The door shuddered as Tiny hit it, squealing furiously. He hit it again, and the center bowed slightly. Vick glanced around. He picked up a disemboweled domestic robot torso and set it on top of the refrigerator, then ran to find something else that was heavy.

As dawn broke an hour later, Vick raced to pile anything and everything against the door. The top hinge had snapped all at once with a dull, brittle *thunk*. The next time Tiny hit the door, it made a different sound, a looser, rattling sound.

Vick spun to face Tara. "*Are you almost done?* Just put together something that *moves.*"

Tara swallowed hard, but otherwise didn't respond.

He turned to Daisy. "Hurry, Daisy. There's no time."

Daisy seemed to understand. At least, she stopped messing with a front shoulder joint and moved on to something else.

Tiny hit the door again; the top buckled out a half inch.

"*Come on, come on.*"

The next time Vick checked on their progress, Daisy

was gone. Vick opened his mouth to ask where she was; then he realized: Tara had merged her into the watchdog. Daisy was the watchdog.

Daisy the watchdog's left front knee flexed. Then her right. She was testing her joints!

Tara circled her, adjusting, tightening, fussing over her like a proud mother. Daisy's new body wasn't pretty. Now that she was finished, she looked more like a wolf than a dog, if a wolf had powerful back legs and smaller, more nimble front legs and could sit up on its haunches like a squirrel. She was the size of a German shepherd and covered in scratched and dented steel plates in a variety of clashing colors that didn't fit neatly together the way Tiny's did. In spots you could see right into her inner workings—a forest of joints, wires, steel supports, and electronics. Her eyes were ridiculously large and bright, like a cartoon animal, set on either side of a long snout packed with steel teeth.

Tara looked at the door, maybe noticing for the first time that it was being battered down. "You might as well open it."

Never in a million years would it have occurred to Vick to help the metal beast get through that door, but if Daisy was ready, what was the point of waiting?

Vick squatted. "Are you ready, Daisy? Do you understand what you have to do? You have to protect us."

Daisy nodded.

Vick pulled a vacuum cleaner off the top of the debris piled in front of the door. He tossed it aside. As he turned to grab something else, Daisy stepped in front of him, gripped the end of the refrigerator at the bottom of the pile, and lifted, sending the entire pile cascading across the roof. She shoved the refrigerator, sending it tumbling into the scattered debris.

Tiny hit the door, and the middle hinge snapped. The only thing holding it now was one of the steel bars Vick had wedged across it. He reached for it.

"Here we go."

Tara took a dozen steps back, positioning herself directly behind Daisy. Vick lifted the bar, let it clatter to the ground, and ran to join Tara.

The next time Tiny hit the door, it slammed to the ground.

Tiny stepped through, followed by Dixie. Dixie's smile faded as she got a look at the new-and-improved Daisy.

She wagged a finger at Vick. "If that walking junkyard so much as scratches Tiny's finish, you're going to be sorry."

Vick's throat was so dry and his heart racing so fast, he wasn't sure he could speak. Tiny was twice Daisy's size, his mouth big enough to swallow Daisy's entire head. Vick brushed his hair out of his eyes and waited.

"I want to know how you got those shop doors open," Dixie said.

"And I want to know where you got that ugly face," Tara shot back.

Vick laughed nervously.

Dixie pointed at Daisy. "Tear it apart."

Tiny charged.

Daisy ran.

"No. Daisy, you have to fight!" Vick shouted as Tiny chased her half a turn around the roof.

Suddenly Daisy stopped, scooped up a three-foot length of water pipe in her squirrel-like front paw, and turned to face the charging Tiny. She swung the pipe and hit Tiny on the side of the face, leaving a big dent. Tiny's eye was sunk deep inside the divot, shattered and unmoving.

Vick punched his fist in the air and whooped with joy.

Tiny lunged at Daisy again; Daisy whacked him in the same spot, further caving in the steel there, then ducked as Tiny swung at her with one of his huge clawed front paws. Daisy spun out of Tiny's reach and landed on all fours, still clutching the pipe.

This time Tiny knew better than to charge. The side of his head was a train wreck, and there was a gap in the seam between the two halves of his head.

"Get her, Tiny," Dixie urged.

Daisy charged right at Tiny. It looked as if they were going to collide headfirst, but at the last instant Daisy jumped, soaring over Tiny's big body lengthwise. She twisted, landing facing Tiny's tail end. Lashing out with one clawed paw, she raked the inside of Tiny's back leg, then retreated out of reach as Tiny spun awkwardly, the leg Daisy had attacked dragging.

Daisy circled the lame watchdog, racing in one direction, and then abruptly changing direction as Tiny tried to keep his good eye on her. Daisy found an opening on Tiny's blind side and struck again, this time at the seam between the inside of Tiny's front leg and his torso. She jumped out of the way just as Tiny's big jaws snapped closed on empty air.

With two limbs damaged, Tiny staggered clumsily. Daisy spun to Tiny's blind side, lunged forward, wedged her claws into the split seam on top of Tiny's head, and pulled as Tiny snapped his jaws, trying to reach her. The seam widened, widened, until the left side of Tiny's head snapped off, exposing a motor shield, orange wires, computer chips, capacitors, and a solar battery. It was the most beautiful sight Vick had ever seen.

"Tiny. *Back*. To me!" Dixie shouted.

Tiny surged backward, dragging Daisy with him.

"Daisy. Stop. That's enough," Tara said. Daisy let go of Tiny's head and backed toward Vick and Tara as Tiny retreated to where Dixie was standing in a corner of the roof.

Vick couldn't believe Tara had called Daisy off. "Why did you do that?"

"She would have *killed* Tiny."

"Tara, it's a *machine*."

Tara just stared past him, her eyes half lidded. Why was he even trying to convince her? When Tara wore her green T-shirt, she was afraid her white one felt lonely and rejected. Whatever. Maybe sending Tiny back to Ms. Alba limping and mangled would make their point better than having him not come back at all.

They stared across the roof at Dixie, who would have to pass them to reach the door.

Finally Tara broke the silence. "Looks like Tiny's finish is going to need a good buffing."

Vick burst out laughing. Tiny looked like he'd been hit by a train.

Dixie stood frozen, knowing if they sicced Daisy on her now, she'd never make it out of the building.

"We don't want a fight, but if you don't leave us alone, we'll send our bodyguard after you, and Ms. Alba, too," Vick said. "And the dude with the stripe."

Dixie opened her mouth to say something, then eyed Daisy and thought better. "Tiny. Come." She stayed close to the edge as she circled toward the doorway, staying as far from Daisy as she could. Tiny staggered after her, one useless back leg banging the steps as they hurried down the stairwell.

"You *better* run!" Tara shouted after Dixie, her hands balled into fists. She reached out and patted Daisy. "Good girl."

Vick eyed Daisy with newfound respect, marveling at how brilliantly she'd fought. She'd figured out that she could hold weapons, and Tiny couldn't, in about two seconds. She'd identified Tiny's weak points just as quickly. How could she know how to do these things? No robot could fight like that without a human directing it.

"You said you didn't know what Daisy could do, because her brain was made from a chip you found in the dump. What chip? What did you salvage it from?"

"I didn't salvage it from anything. I found it the other day. You were there. Remember? You told me to stop screwing around with it and keep digging."

He remembered. "You said it was weird."

"It *is* weird. I don't get it at all."

And now the entire dump was sectioned off, and an army of people working for a watchdog kingpin were sifting through it.

Did you find it yet? Ms. Alba had asked Stripe.

His heart shifted gears, pounding slow and hard. "You found it right on top, didn't you? You barely had to dig."

"That's right. How did you know that?"

"Because it had just been dumped. Someone threw it out by accident, and Ms. Alba is combing the entire dump to get it back. Because it's something special."

Tara put her hand over her mouth. "Oh my gosh. That's got to be it."

Daisy picked up the shear cutters and a spool of twenty-two-gauge wire and began working on her own knee, either fixing a flaw or improving her new body. Vick looked on, mesmerized. Tara saw what she was doing and went to help.

CHAPTER 9

Four hours later, both Tara and Daisy seemed satisfied. Tara flopped down beside Vick, who was lying on an old carpet. He'd napped and watched them work on and off. Daisy disappeared through the doorway that led downstairs. She looked better—her seams were tighter, and she moved more quietly—no metal parts rubbing together. She still resembled the world's ugliest patchwork quilt, though—her parts had come from a bunch of domestic bots, which came in all different colors.

Off in the distance, an ambulance wailed.

"We have to get out of here," Vick said. "They'll come back."

"What's the difference where we go? They'll know right where we are."

Vick jolted upright. He'd forgotten about the tracers in their arms.

"Don't worry. Daisy will protect us," Tara said.

"She can't protect us from everything. They might have guns." Vick regretted the words as soon as he said them and tried to walk himself back. "They'll probably leave us alone."

Tara stared at him, wide-eyed. "Except they won't. They're not the sort of people who think, 'Okay, we're even.' They'll just keep coming after us, and coming after us."

They had to get those tracers out of their arms. Only, they weren't big things you just take out, they were chips small enough to travel through the tip of a needle.

So why had East run off so quickly? Why hadn't she been afraid of Tiny coming after *her*?

Vick smiled. Because she and her friends stole domestic robots, and all domestic robots had tracers. They must know how to deactivate them.

He stood. "We have to find East. She can get rid of these tracers."

"You think?"

"*Daisy,*" Vick called. Daisy appeared on the fire escape ladder. "We're taking a trip."

The problem was, Vick had no idea where East lived. It wasn't like he could look up her address in a directory. All he could think to do was walk around and ask people, even though he hated talking to strangers on the street.

It was getting dark. Normally they avoided the streets like the plague after dark, but with Daisy around, Vick felt a wonderful sense of freedom. The scary-looking people who hung out on the street corners at night didn't look very scary with Daisy at their side.

After a few blocks Daisy began to range farther from them, doing little reconnaissance trips the way she'd done when she was nothing but a wee bot.

She waited outside while they went into Peary Pawn.

Mert, the shop owner, raised her white eyebrows when she saw who it was. "A little late for the two of you to be out, don't you think?"

Vick explained who they were looking for, leaving out a lot of the details of why.

Mert had no idea. "There are probably fifty chop shops like that in this city. Most are south of here, but you don't want to go anywhere near that part of town."

Sharing a half box of saltines Mert gave them, they headed south. Vick knew the odds of finding one person in an entire city were close to zero, but he didn't know what else to do. They had to find East.

Before long they hit a sacrifice zone, where huge mounds of twisted steel beams and concrete blocked their way, and they had to skirt around it. Some parts of the city had gotten so broken down, they just knocked down all the buildings. Supposedly, the city was going to clear it all out someday and build parks or something.

As they turned a corner, they nearly bumped into three guys, all with long hair bleached ghost-white.

The one in the middle, who was tall and stocky, held out a gloved hand. "Whoa, what are you munchkins doing on my street?"

Vick looked around. Daisy had chosen a bad time to go on one of her jaunts. "Just looking for someone. Do you know a girl named East?"

"What do I look like, the Yellow Pages?" The big man curled his fingers at Vick. "Give me the backpack and empty your pockets. Your girlfriend, too."

"I'm his sister, not his girlfriend." Tara balled her hands into fists, turned her face toward the sky, and shouted, "Daisy!"

The big guy looked at his friends. They all burst out laughing. "Daisy? Who's she, your big sister?" He put his hands on his hips. "Don't make me tell you again. Backpack. Pockets."

Vick heard the click of Daisy's claws on the sidewalk.

He could tell the exact moment she appeared around the corner behind them, because all three of the guys' faces went as white as their hair.

"This is our big sister, Daisy," Vick said.

Mr. Tough Guy swallowed. "Where the hell did you get that?"

"The watchdog store. They were having a sale," Tara said.

Vick was enjoying this. So much. For the last eight months guys like these had terrorized them. He loved seeing them looking like they might wet their pants.

"Like I said before, we're looking for a girl named East. She's a Brumby, hangs out with some other kids who run a chop shop. They make watchdogs."

The guys exchanged glances, shrugged, and shook their heads at each other. "Don't know her."

Vick folded his arms. "Well, I'm sure you know *someone* who knows her, since you own this street and all. You got a phone?"

The guy reached into his back pocket. Daisy leaned forward and made a deep clicking sound until he showed her it was only a phone.

"How about you two?" Vick asked.

The other guys produced phones as well.

"Good. Now, call all of your friends until you find someone who knows East."

They started dialing. Vick and Tara leaned against the wall as the three of them talked into their phones.

"This is so cool," Tara said. "After this let's make them dance."

Not ten minutes into their phone marathon, the guy on the left turned to Vick. "This girl East. She was gone for a while, just got back?"

"That's her."

"Their shop's in an abandoned church on West Chestnut."

After thanking the men for their help, Vick and Tara walked away laughing.

"This is so great," Tara said.

Vick looked to their watchdog, who was click-clacking along behind them. He wondered if, with all her skills, she had GPS or an internal map, too. "Thanks, Daisy. Can you show us how to get to this church?"

Daisy nodded and took the lead.

Tara was right. This was so cool.

CHAPTER 10

The church was called Saint Boniface. It was a big red-brick building with two bell towers. The tall wooden front doors were unlocked.

The chapel was a long, cavernous hall with a high curved ceiling. It wasn't hard to see it had once been gorgeous. Now it was strewn with trash, the walls crowded with graffiti.

"East?" Vick called.

No answer. Maybe the white-haired guy had been lying. Then it occurred to him: he was doing this the hard way. He turned to Daisy. "See if there are any people here."

Daisy loped off.

Vick went to sit in one of the pews, but the benches were caked in dust and fallen plaster. He set his and Tara's packs on the floor between the pews and waited for Daisy to return.

"I like it here." Tara was staring at the ceiling.

"I don't. It feels like the roof could collapse any minute. And it's creepy."

"It's not creepy, it's peaceful."

Daisy appeared through an archway to the side of the big hall.

"Did you find anyone?" Vick asked.

Daisy nodded, and turned back the way she'd come. She led them down a staircase to a hallway lined with Sunday school classrooms and offices, then down a second, narrower flight of stairs into another hallway that was completely dark except for a sliver of light filtering out from under a door.

Vick rapped on it, the steel door stinging his knuckles. "East? It's Vick and Tara."

On the other side of the door a steel bar slid out of place. Locks clicked. It swung open a few inches, and East's face appeared, her hair a halo of dark curls now that it wasn't tied back with a rubber band. She looked amused and a little stunned. "How did you *find* me?" Then she noticed Daisy, and her eyes widened. "Is that yours?"

"Mm-hm. Tara built her."

East opened the door wider. She was dressed in a sleeveless black T-shirt over oil-stained jeans. "No wonder Alba snatched her up." She stepped out to take a closer look at Daisy.

Two other people appeared in the doorway: a black guy who looked about fifteen, with his arms covered in tattoos and an aluminum bat in one hand, and a skinny black kid with big eyes who was around five. Vick recognized the older guy immediately. He was one of the jerks who'd pounded on their fire escape, laughing and saying he was coming to get them.

"That's my little brother, North, and that's Rando," East said.

"Who are you?" Rando let the bat sag to the floor, though he didn't look happy to see strangers at his door.

"Vick. And this is Tara. We were stuck in the sweatshop with East."

East turned. "They're the ones who got me *out*. Where's the little one that broke us out? You still got her?"

Tara rested her hand on Daisy's head. "She's right here."

Vick explained what had happened as East's eyes grew wider and wider. While he told the story, another kid appeared in the doorway—the white guy with long dreadlocks. He looked to be about fourteen, with a neck like a linebacker's. The other guy who'd terrorized them that night. East said his name was Torch.

"I think I can guess why you went to all this trouble to track me down," East said when Vick finished his story. "The tracers, right?"

"Can you get them out?" Vick asked.

"We can deactivate them, yeah. Come on, let's get it done before you lead Alba right to my door." East led them into a long, low-ceilinged basement with cots along one wall, moldy hymnals piled on a beat-up piano, and a curtain drawn to reveal a shower and toilet toward the back. In the center were low benches piled with shop equipment, electronics, and robot parts.

Torch grunted with disgust and moved to the far end of the basement.

"What's your problem?" East asked.

He wrinkled his nose. "They smell like garbage. So does their watchdog."

East put her hands on her hips. "I don't know if you've noticed, but you don't smell too good yourself."

"Compared to them I smell like freaking rose petals."

East closed her eyes for a second, shook her head. "Rando, can you fix them up?"

Rando sauntered to one of the benches and retrieved a steel wand. "Fifty bucks each."

East cursed under her breath. "They *helped* me. They got me out of there, which is more than I can say for *you*."

Rando shrugged. "So? They got you out. They didn't do nothing for me. And I'm the one with the equipment."

East huffed in frustration. "Fine. I'll owe you. *Twenty* each."

"Okay. Your credit's good." Rando beckoned Tara over with his fingertip. "You first, come on. Which arm?"

When Tara pointed to her left arm, Rando turned her so her left shoulder was facing him. He ran the wand over it. "All set. Now you."

Vick felt a huge sense of relief as Rando ran the cold steel wand over his shoulder. Now he was truly free of Ms. Alba and Dixie. While Rando worked, East and Torch circled Daisy, sometimes bending to examine a detail up close.

"It's rough, but it's gorgeous, considering what you had to work with." East looked at Tara. "You did this all yourself?"

"Not all," Tara said.

"Vick helped you?"

Tara shook her head. "Daisy."

Torch let out a harsh laugh. He had bulgy fish eyes, and when he smiled his gums showed, along with way too many teeth. "Right. Your watchdog helped design herself. And then she wrote a book while farting 'Jingle Bells.'"

"Hey, Daisy?" Vick scanned their workbench. There was a half-finished raccoon-sized watchdog laid out. "Can you fix that?"

Daisy went over and examined the watchdog for a moment. Vick felt a warm rush of anticipation. It was going to feel so good to shut this guy's big mouth after what he'd done at the roof.

Daisy picked up a portable band saw and got to work.

Vick turned to Torch. "You want her to fart 'Jingle Bells' while she works?"

Torch couldn't take his eyes off Daisy. "That's got to be a trick. How the hell can a watchdog make a watchdog?"

"Tara's a genius when it comes to electronics," Vick said.

"Bull." Torch gestured at Daisy. "No little Brumby girl designed that thing's brain out of dump salvage. How are you getting it to do that?"

Vick hesitated. He wasn't sure he trusted these people enough to tell them the truth.

"Come on, Vick. We're on the same side," East said. "If Alba has her way, we'll all be living in her sweatshop before long."

Still, Vick hesitated. He didn't like Rando and Torch. He didn't trust them. They'd shown what sort of guys they were, rattling that fire escape while Tara screamed.

They both had that walk, the same as every other kid who thought he was tough: arms out away from their sides, swaying, a little bounce at the end of each step. Vick wondered if they practiced in front of the mirror. All of Vick's friends just *walked*. They didn't try to walk cool, or tough, they just *walked*.

His former friends, Vick reminded himself. He hadn't heard from any of them in months. Although it was hard to keep in touch with someone who had no phone, no address, and whose only Internet access was at the public library.

Torch was standing over Daisy, watching her work. "You know what? I could care less where she came from. What can we *use* her for, besides working on watchdogs? That's what I want to know."

Tara put her hands on her hips. "She's not yours. She's ours."

Torch raised his hands. "I said 'we.' We includes you. I mean, Rando just helped you out, didn't he?"

"East helped us out," Vick said. "Rando wanted fifty bucks to do something that took him ten seconds." He decided it was time to lay all the cards on the table, so everyone knew where they stood. "He also pounded on the bottom of our fire escape and yelled that he was coming to get us."

East frowned. "Huh? What are you talking about?"

Torch pointed at Vick. "That was *you*?" He threw back his head and laughed.

"Aw, we were just screwing with you," Rando said.

"What did they do?" East looked from Rando to Vick.

Tara wrapped her arms around herself as Vick recounted what had happened that night.

"You scared us," Tara said when Vick finished. "You shouldn't laugh about it, buttheads."

East was shaking her head. "Unbelievable. You guys are pigs." She looked at Vick. "I'm really sorry."

Vick just shrugged. He felt uncomfortable in that shop, surrounded by stolen property.

"Hang out awhile. You want something to eat?" East asked.

"I'm really hungry. Starving," Tara said before Vick could answer. She looked around. "Do you have quesadillas?"

"We don't have much of anything. Times being tough and all." Torch raised a finger. "Hey, I have an idea. Why don't you ask your watchdog to find some food? If he's so danged smart, that should be a snap."

"He's a she," Tara said.

Vick narrowed his eyes. "What do you mean by 'find'? Where do you 'find' food?"

Torch folded his arms, which made his biceps bulge even more. "Fine. *Steal.* Why don't you get her to *steal* some food?"

Vick shook his head. "We don't steal."

Rando grunted a laugh and rolled his eyes. "Seriously? You think we're bad guys because we steal? People on their way to the all-you-can-eat buffet look right through us when we ask for help, but *we're* the bad guys?" He turned away. "That's messed up."

"Could she steal quesadillas?" Tara asked.

Vick was so hungry. Plus, he liked the idea of giving East something to repay her for the forty dollars she'd laid out. "I don't think we can give her a grocery list."

"Okay. But I hope she brings quesadillas."

There was a knot in Vick's stomach as he approached Daisy, who was still working on the watchdog. "Daisy, can you find us something to eat?"

Daisy nodded and set down the needle-nose pliers she'd been using. East unlocked and opened the door, and Daisy headed off.

Vick perched on a stool beside the workbench. "What if she hurts someone?"

"Anyone stupid enough to get in her way deserves to get hurt," Torch said.

Vick ignored the comment. "We'll share anything Daisy brings back with you," he said to East. He looked pointedly at Torch, hoping he got the message that the same wasn't necessarily true for him. He might have to grovel a little first.

They quickly ran out of topics of conversation, now that everyone couldn't circle around Daisy and talk about her hip joints. Vick leaned against one of the workbenches and stared at a cupcake wrapper on the floor.

"Do you like *Dinotrux*?" North, the little kid, asked. He was sitting on a mattress, looking at Vick. His dark, curly hair was short but uneven; it was pretty obvious East had cut it.

"Me? I guess. I used to play the video game when I was about seven." It had been old even then, but Vick could see why North was drawn toward a TV show about robot dinosaurs.

"Who's your favorite Dinotrux? Mine's Revvit."

The name was familiar, but he couldn't remember what Revvit looked like. It had been a long time since he'd thought about Dinotrux.

The door swung open. Daisy headed straight for Vick, lowered her head, and opened her mouth.

A pile of dead pigeons spilled out.

Torch and Rando burst out laughing.

"Mmmmmm, my mouth is watering, just looking at them." Torch picked up one of the dead pigeons and held it in Vick's face. "Eat up, sport."

Vick knocked the pigeon away, his face burning with embarrassment. "I told her to find food, so she found food. I didn't tell her what kind of food." He got right up in Daisy's big silver face and looked into her big cartoon eyes, his nose almost touching the end of her long pointed snout. "We need food that's already cooked. Do you understand?"

Daisy nodded.

"Don't hurt anyone. Even if it means you can't get the food. Understand?"

Daisy nodded again.

"Hang on." Rando went to a plastic cabinet set on one of the workbenches, opened one of its tiny drawers, and fished something out. He slapped it onto Daisy's haunch, then handed Vick a video card. "Portable camera. Now you can follow the action."

As Daisy disappeared up the stairs, Vick watched the card. She trotted through the church, turned right out the door without hesitating, and headed up North Noble Street.

When she reached a sidewalk café on the corner, Daisy paused. Diners in the cordoned-off outdoor area, all khakis and black dresses and shiny shoes, eyed Daisy, their forks frozen in midair.

Daisy turned back, then headed up the crossing street and down an alley that ran behind the café, where there was a door leading into the kitchen.

Everyone was gathered around Vick, watching the screen. When Daisy clacked into the kitchen, a cook standing over a grill shouted in surprise.

"What is *that* doing in here?" a woman who looked like she might be the manager asked as Daisy clinked past.

Daisy took a plastic takeout bag from a pile, letting the rest slide to the floor. She went to a long counter where steaming plates of food were waiting to be picked up by waiters. As café workers looked on, dumbfounded, she dumped the contents of the first plate into the bag. Shouts of surprise and anger rose as Daisy went down the line until all the plates were empty, and the bag was full. No one tried to stop her, although the woman who might be the manager was on the phone, probably calling the police. Daisy put the handle of the bag in her mouth and trotted out into the alley.

Ten minutes later she was at the door with the bag. Tara gave her a huge hug and a kiss. Vick was tempted to do the same as he accepted the warm bag from her. The food was a steaming stew of sandwiches, casseroles, vegetables, cake, and . . . quesadillas. No one complained, because there was a ton of it. Daisy had swiped about a dozen plates.

As soon as she finished eating, Tara made a beeline to the workbench, where she took advantage of the wide assortment of tools to mess around with Daisy's design, as Daisy looked on. North went over to watch.

"We gotta get going in a couple of minutes," Vick called to Tara. He didn't want her to get too comfortable. Rando and Torch were standing off near the door, talking, watching Daisy with their bellies full. They would like nothing better than for Vick and Tara to get comfortable, while they thought of uses for Daisy, and ways to steal her away from them.

"Can I touch her?" North asked Tara.

"Sure," Tara said.

North ran his hand along Daisy's side. "Can you play with her?"

Tara looked around, grabbed a filthy welcome mat from under the workbench, and dropped it onto Daisy's back like a saddle, covering a section of her jagged steel armor. She patted the mat. "Climb on."

East grimaced, then shouted, "Be careful!" as Tara helped North mount the ragged, fierce-looking watchdog. Once North was on, he leaned forward and grasped Daisy's neck.

"Can you give him a ride?" Tara asked Daisy.

Daisy took a few tentative steps. North cackled gleefully, so Daisy took a few more, moving more quickly.

"We're in the same boat, you and me." East was standing beside Vick, arms folded. She and North had the same dimples, the same sharp cheekbones.

"Which boat is that?"

"We both have family to take care of."

Vick couldn't argue with that, although in some ways it was Tara who was taking care of him. "Sometimes when I talk to her I hear myself saying things my mom used to say to us."

East laughed. "'Don't jump on the bed.' 'Wash your hands.' 'Stop picking your nose.'"

"There's no room here," Tara called. It was true—Daisy was doing her best, but there wasn't much space for her to run. "Let's go upstairs. Come on, Daisy." Tara ran to open the door.

East stood. "Come on, Mom, we better keep an eye on the kids."

Vick followed her out. At least upstairs they'd be closer to the exit. North could get his ride; then they could say goodbye.

Up in the main chapel, Daisy cut loose, racing around the pews, her movements so smooth North barely bounced on the makeshift saddle.

"Listen," East said as they watched, "I know you have good reason to hate Rando and Torch. They can be idiots. But the whole time I was in Alba's sweatshop, they took care of North. They fed him, even paid for a doctor one time when he got a respiratory infection. When you strip away all the immature antics, they're good guys."

Vick pictured the pair, who'd been watching some show about a psycho clown trying to escape from a prison circus when they left. He tried to imagine liking them, but all he could see were two guys who would be school bullies if they were still in school.

"I'll keep it in mind."

East nodded. "Like I said before, we're on the same side. 'The enemy of my enemy is my friend,' you know? You've got a big-time beast who can protect us. We know the streets, and we know Alba."

Vick didn't say anything. He had no interest in teaming up with these people, or anyone else. He just wanted to be left alone and have nobody bother them. Now that they had Daisy, they could count on those things.

East was watching him, studying him. "If Alba comes at you for messing up Tiny, she'll come at you like a wrecking ball. You're going to need friends."

"Okay." He'd had friends, when his mom was still alive and he was in school. He wasn't sure where they were now . . . probably playing video games and munching on chocolate-covered pretzels in their air-conditioned bedrooms. He waved a hand to get Tara's attention. "We better get going."

Tara put her hands on her hips. "Going *where*?"

"To find a new place to live. We need to get set up so we can get some sleep." Which would entail dumping their laundry on the floor and lying down on it.

Tara helped North down, and they said goodbye.

"Remember what I said," East said as Vick and Tara headed for the street, with Daisy following.

A knot of tension in Vick's neck and shoulders relaxed as they reached the sidewalk.

"Why couldn't we stay there?" Tara asked.

"Because (a) they didn't invite us, (b) they're criminals, and (c) those two guys were looking at Daisy like she was a Christmas present someone left under their tree."

Tara stared at a billboard advertisement for a new action movie plastered on the side of a passing bus as if she hadn't heard him.

"You can count on me, I can count on you, and we can both count on Daisy," Vick said. "We can't count on Uncle Mason and Aunt Ruby, or our friends, or those thugs carving up stolen robots. We watch out for each other, and we keep to ourselves." He choked up, because that was the truth. All he had was Tara and Daisy.

"I'm glad Daisy's one of the people we can count on, because when we only had each other, we ended up in a sweatshop."

Vick barked a laugh. "Smart aleck."

He asked Daisy to scout around and find them a place to sleep, maybe an apartment in an abandoned building. Daisy took off.

Before they'd had Daisy they didn't dare sleep indoors where people like Rando and Torch could stumble on them, but with Daisy watching over them they could sleep wherever they wanted.

"Now that we have Daisy, things are going to turn around."

"Because she can steal food for us?" Tara asked.

The question made Vick sting with guilt. "That's only for emergencies. We need to figure out ways we can use her to earn money legally. Enough to rent a real apartment."

"With royal blue carpet and shell tile in the kitchen. And a white concrete birdbath in the backyard in the corner by the water recycler?"

"Yes. Just as good as the one we lived in with Mom." It felt good to be able to say that.

"Only, without Mom."

Vick's throat tightened. "I can learn to cook all the foods you love, and we'll have movie nights where we throw all the pillows and couch cushions on the floor and lie in them, the way we used to."

"I'd like that." She looked a few feet to Vick's right. "You're a good brother. A lot of brothers with a sister like me would have ditched her at a shelter by now."

"You know I'd never do that to you. You're stuck with me."

Could kids rent an apartment? Vick didn't know. Maybe he could pay some homeless adult to pretend to be their parent. First, though, he had to figure out how Daisy could make them some money.

CHAPTER 11

On a Saturday afternoon, the sidewalk outside the Planet Lucky Gambling Emporium was like a street fair, with vendors selling everything from fedoras to super-caffeinated fruit juice, and card tables set up by small-time operators offering every sort of game of chance, most of them probably fixed.

There weren't many kids around, but the looks they got as they crossed the street were probably because they had a watchdog with them, not because they were kids. It seemed like everyone was suddenly interested in watchdogs, the same way some people were fascinated by jacked-up trucks and sports cars with flames painted on the sides. Something about custom machines got people's blood pumping.

As soon as they took up a spot along the sidewalk and Vick told Daisy to sit down, people started coming up to look at her. He'd been awake half the night worrying about how two kids would get a bunch of grown-up gamblers' attention. It turned out to be no problem at all.

A guy with slicked-back hair wearing an old white suit leaned in close to Daisy's face. "What sort of programming does she have?"

"It's all custom work," Vick said, trying to sound older than he was.

"You looking to sell her?" the guy asked. He said it like he didn't care one way or another.

Tara huffed and started to speak (even though Vick had asked her over and over to let him handle this). Vick spoke over her. "We're just showing her off a little."

"I'll bet you fifty dollars my watchdog can clean up all the trash around here," Tara blurted.

Vick wanted to scream. He'd planned this all out, how he was going to move the conversation around to the trash and lead up to the bet, all the time acting like a dumb sucker kid.

The man chuckled at Tara and ran his hand through his greased hair. "That's a nice piece of work, little lady, but as far as I can see it's still a robot."

Vick had thought long and hard about what sort of bet he could win with Daisy. Clearing trash was easy for people, but impossible for a bot. Too many decisions without clear rules to follow. You could tell them to throw out everything on the ground that was not a person or a chair—they could do that just fine, but don't ask them to figure out what was trash and what was someone's coffee they'd set on the ground beside their chair between sips.

Vick pinched his chin, trying to look like a sucker. "I don't know, I think she might be able to. She's awfully smart."

Laughing, the man turned to an older guy sitting behind a nearby table. "Hey, Jay, you hear this? Their watchdog can clean up all the trash for us. What do you think?"

"Bud, I think I'd better hang on to my shoes or they'll end up in the trash."

Others nearby laughed at the crack.

"Oh yeah?" Tara said. "I'll bet you she can do it. A hundred bucks."

Bud stopped smiling. "Let me see your hundred dollars."

Vick folded his arms to keep his hands from shaking. "We'll put up our watchdog against your hundred."

Jay, the old guy behind the table, stood. "I'll take that bet."

Bud took a step toward Jay's table. "It's my bet. They offered it to me."

Jay raised his hands and sat back down. "Fine. It's your bet." He didn't look happy about it, though. He was going to feel a whole lot better about it in a couple of minutes.

"We need a moderator here," Bud called, while he waved like he was flagging a taxi.

A large woman with graying hair hurried over. "I'll do it. What are you betting?"

Bud tilted his head and smiled. "These young people here believe their watchdog can clean up all the trash, and only the trash, in this area. I'm betting a hundred dollars against their watchdog that it can't."

The woman looked at Vick. "You sure you want to make that bet?"

"Yes." A hundred dollars. Man, could they use a hundred dollars.

The woman tilted her head and gave Vick a long look. "All right, then." She put one hand on her hip, and then pointed out the area that would be included in the wager. No one seemed to notice that Daisy was watching with interest, acting nothing like a dumb bot. "My word is final on whether something is trash, and my fee is five dollars, paid by the winner."

Vick nodded. So did Bud.

"Here you go." Jay held out a plastic bag to put the trash in. He gave Vick a look like *You poor little stupid kid* as Vick thanked him.

"Let's go, then." The moderator folded her arms.

Tara took the bag from Vick and squatted next to Daisy. She handed Daisy the bag. "You know what to do. Sorry we couldn't think up something more dignified to bet on."

Daisy accepted the bag. This being Chicago, the ground was littered with wrappers, Styrofoam cups, a smashed phone, even a ratty sneaker with half the sole gone. Daisy started in one corner of the area the woman had pointed out. As she approached Jay's table, Vick could see Bud grin. Jay had set his beat-up phone down beside his chair.

"I want you to remember this," Jay said to Bud. He'd done it on purpose.

Daisy picked up the phone, sat on her haunches, examined it to see that it worked, and set it back down.

"Wait a minute." Bud was scowling, suddenly not enjoying himself so much.

Daisy scanned the surface of Jay's table, then lifted a Styrofoam coffee cup and looked into it. There was a half inch of coffee in it. She set it back down, then picked up the Snickers candy bar wrapper sitting beside it and tossed it in the bag.

"Go, Daisy!" Tara jumped up and down, her arms raised in the air.

When the discarded sneaker went into the bag, Bud had seen enough. He pointed at Vick. "They're cheating."

"How are they cheating?" the moderator asked. She didn't sound skeptical, more like she desperately wanted to know how Daisy was doing what she was doing.

Bud sputtered. "I don't know exactly. No watchdog can do what that one is doing. Maybe one of their friends is hiding in there."

A small crowd had formed. They muttered in astonishment, and cried out in surprise as Daisy tossed the smashed phone into the bag.

"Hundred dollars. Hundred dollars," Tara sang.

Daisy paused at a piece of gum partially stuck to the pavement. She looked up at Vick.

"No coaching!" Bud shouted. "It's a forfeit if you coach."

Daisy looked at Bud before plucking up the gum and dropping it in the bag, just to be safe. Vick was certain if Daisy could make facial expressions she would have been glaring at him.

When the area was spotless, Daisy handed the bag to Vick.

"Hundred dollars. Hundred dollars," Tara sang louder.

"Hang on," the woman said. "I want to take a look at your watchdog." She bent close to Daisy and moved her head from side to side, trying to see into Daisy's seams to make sure there wasn't a kid crouched in there. Finally she straightened. "It's a robot."

"Then how can it do what it just did?" Bud asked.

"You got me. But you owe them a hundred dollars."

Bud folded his arms, making no attempt to reach into his pocket.

"Daisy, that man owes us a hundred dollars," Tara said.

Daisy walked over to Bud, and then rose on her hind legs until her face was inches from his. The awful metal-scraping-metal sound of her growl rose from deep in her throat.

Bud took out his wallet, counted out a hundred dollars, and handed it to Vick.

Vick paid the woman her five, and then they left, skipping down the street, both of them singing, "Hundred dollars, hundred dollars" and laughing like crazy.

With real money in his pocket for the first time since Mom had died, passing faces seemed friendlier, and colors seemed brighter. All these months he'd been telling Tara they could lift themselves out of the mess they were in, but he hadn't really believed it, not deep down. Now he did.

He reached over and patted Tara's back. "You did it. You saved us. I'm so proud of you. Mom would be, too."

Tara gave him a big wide grin. "Now I want to have some fun."

"What kind of fun?"

Tara threw her hands in the air. "Real fun. Like we used to." She ticked ideas off on her fingers. "Cubs game. Art Institute. Ferris wheel. Mini golf. Buckingham Fountain."

That sounded so great to Vick, but some of those things were probably really expensive.

"How about just the Ferris wheel and the fountain?"

Tara shook her head emphatically. "All of it. A downtown fun day, like we used to have with Mom."

"But we don't want to spend all the money we just made!"

"We won't spend all of it. Just some of it." She grabbed his arm and pulled. "Come on."

"You're pulling me the wrong way. Wrigley Field is that way." At least, he thought it was. He was pretty sure it was a long way off. They'd have to take the el.

Vick felt nervous about spending so much money when they'd barely had enough to eat for the past few months, but now that they had Daisy, it wasn't like they had to worry about going hungry. And maybe they could pull the same stunt outside the gambling emporium a couple more times before word got around. By then Vick would have to come up with another way to make money with Daisy.

CHAPTER 12

Heading into the nice part of the city was like traveling forward through time. In the ghettos there were no robots, and the buildings were dingy, the brick blackened by pollution. As they crossed West Fullerton on the el, there was less brick and steel, more carbon fiber, the clean, colorful buildings twisting and swooping into the sky like they were made of taffy. By the time they reached North Avenue, most people Vick saw out the window of the train had domestic robots trailing them. Some of the robots resembled people; a few were even dressed in human clothes. Others walked on all fours or sixes, like big, colorful cartoon bugs. Most of the vehicles were sleek, auto-driven jobs that looked like they were made of colored ice. Inside a passing shop Vick could see waist-high munchkin robots scurrying around.

The day they were kicked out of their apartment, Vick had headed toward this part of town, because it was safe here. There were lots of police around, both public and private. A half hour after Vick and Tara had arrived, they were picked up by the police. Vick had been so relieved. He'd thought they were saved, that the police would help them. The police drove them to the bad part of town and dropped them off in front of a shelter. Vick could still see the policewoman's face as she opened the cruiser's rear door to let them out, her eyes bored as she told them they'd have somewhere to sleep in that part of town.

"I feel much better here." Tara was watching out the el's window in the seat next to Vick. "The inside of my head always feels like whatever I'm looking at. When we're in the dump, it feels like garbage; when we're here, it feels neat and clean."

Vick grinned at that. Tara had an odd way of putting things sometimes, but he understood what she was saying. "I'm glad you thought of it." The train slowed. "Here's our stop." Vick glanced to the back of the car where Daisy was squatting in the robot storage area. He signaled that this was their stop. Daisy nodded.

Moments later they were on the clean streets of Grant Park. Tara raced past the twin lion statues that book-ended the entrance to the Art Institute, reciting at high volume, "*American Gothic* by Grant Wood. *Nighthawks* by Edward Hopper. *Paris Street; Rainy Day* by Gustav Caillebotte. *Yellow Hickory Leaves with Daisy* by Georgia O'Keeffe . . ."

Vick was relieved to see that kids under fourteen were only five dollars each. The guards didn't say a word about Daisy as they passed through the entrance. A few other people had domestic robots with them, pushing carriages or just following them.

Vick followed Tara as she headed toward the first work on her list. She always visited the same paintings, and it was exactly that—visiting. To Tara, the paintings were just as alive as her T-shirts and Chloe. Each painting was a friend. Sometimes Vick envied her imagination.

"Hello, *American Gothic* by Grant Wood." She waved at *American Gothic,* and moved on excitedly to the next painting on her list. She'd hated going to the Art Institute until Mom got her to make a list of the paintings she was going to see. Once she had that list, she couldn't wait.

Vick's chest got tight, remembering the trips they'd taken there with Mom. Mom hadn't graduated from high school, but she'd always pushed them to do "smart" things—visit museums, see plays instead of movies. She loved trashy romance books, but her rule for herself was she had to read one classic—*Moby-Dick* or *Jane Eyre*— for every trashy romance she read. No matter how boring the book turned out to be, she read every word.

Daisy had to wait outside Wrigley Field while they watched the Cubs game. Tara cheered wildly for the Cubs. She didn't know any of the players; she just liked to cheer. She especially liked it when the crowd did "the wave." Noise and chaos bothered a lot of people with autism, but it had never bothered Tara, as long as it was happy noise and happy chaos.

The wheel on the Navy Pier had big, roomy gondola cars, and there was no line and plenty of empty space, so when Tara asked if Daisy could ride with them, the ticket-taker waved her on without a word.

The ride cost twenty-four precious dollars, but while they glided along, the lake on one side, the city on the other, Vick felt like a normal kid. It was like the hunger and cold, the threats and taunts from people on the streets, had all been a bad dream. When the ride ended, Tara was hopping around like she had to go to the bathroom as they wandered toward Grant Park.

"This is the best day. Cubs win. One hundred paintings. Ten revolutions on the Ferris wheel. An epic day."

Vick couldn't argue. He felt like he was walking on

air. He took in the fountain up ahead, three tiers of water cascading and spraying into the air surrounded by bronze sea monsters. With Daisy watching over them they could finally come out of the shadows. One way or another, there would be more money coming in. If Vick couldn't think of anything else, Daisy could always repair electronics day and night. Maybe they could start that business Vick had been thinking about, buying broken TVs and stuff and fixing them to resell. They would rent an apartment. Maybe next fall they could go back to school.

"Last stop of the day. Buckingham Fountain." Tara's gaze suddenly shifted. "*Ooh.* Italian ice." She pointed at a silver cart with a red-and-white umbrella, where a silver-faced robot was scooping Italian ice into paper cups. "I want raspberry." She ran toward the cart.

"Come on, Daisy. Looks like we're getting Italian ice." Vick jogged after Tara, soaking up her good cheer like it was a vitamin he was deficient in.

In short order, Tara's mouth was blue. Vick tipped his paper cup and drank down some of the melted juice, knowing his own mouth was a smear of orange.

An old man, his spine bent so badly he had to crane his neck to look straight ahead, shuffled toward them. He held out his hand as he drew close.

"We don't have any money." Usually one look at Vick

was enough to tell people that he couldn't afford to give handouts.

"No. I'm supposed to give you this." The old man raised his hand higher. Now Vick saw he was holding a plastic, wafer-thin phone.

"Who is it from?"

"From the lady who's gonna call you on it." The old man shoved the phone toward Vick. "Just take it so I can go home."

Vick accepted the phone. As he studied it, it rang. Before Vick could decide what he wanted to do, the screen expanded to the size of a sheet of paper. Ms. Alba's face filled it.

"Do you understand how much trouble you're in? I mean, do you fully grasp it?"

The question caught Vick off guard. "Just leave us alone. We're not bothering you."

He looked around for Tara. She was over by the fountain.

"You're not bothering me? You mean, besides stealing from me?"

"We didn't steal anything—" Vick closed his mouth. He'd been wondering if she'd figured out they had the chip. That answered his question.

"One of my friends caught your act outside the Emporium," she said. "Cute." Her face was like a mask. She showed no expression at all—just a cool, controlled, businesslike neutral. And Vick suddenly remembered that *he* had orange lips. "Here's the deal. Give me my chip, and you get a full pardon. None of my people will bother you. They'll spread the word that you're under my protection."

Once she had the chip and Daisy was gone, Ms. Alba would take them back to the sweatshop, or worse. Vick had no doubt. Who would be dumb enough to trust a woman who imprisoned kids in a sweatshop?

Vick licked his dry lips and tried to sound cool and calm. "You know what? I'm going to go with no."

Ms. Alba tilted her head, just a hint of annoyance seeping into her tone. "Little boy, one way or another I'm getting that chip back. Are you *sure* you don't want to do it so we walk away as friends?"

"I'm sure." Vick put on his best cheery tone. "You have a nice day now. Buh-bye." He disconnected and stuffed the phone into his pocket. Suddenly he felt terribly exposed standing in the square.

He raced over to Daisy, who was halfway between him and Tara, ever watching. "Time to find our new home. Watch for danger. The people who want to hurt us know where we are."

Daisy nodded.

"Tara," Vick called. "We have to get going."

Tara ignored him, or didn't hear him. She was staring up at the water cascading down the three tiers of the fountain.

"*Tara,*" Vick called louder.

This time she turned. Vick waved for her to come over. Her shoulders slumped, but she headed toward him. "What's your rush?"

Daisy took a few steps in the opposite direction and growled—steel grinding against steel.

Vick looked past Daisy with a sinking dread.

A watchdog stood across the square, alone, waiting. It was the grizzly from Ms. Alba's sweatshop—a jet-black steel hulk, even bigger than Tiny.

Ms. Alba's black Maserati was parked at the curb beyond it.

The grizzly let out a metallic squeal and charged at Tara as bystanders, shouting in surprise and alarm, cleared out.

Daisy bolted to intercept the grizzly.

The two watchdogs collided; Daisy was knocked backward by the force of the much bigger grizzly but stayed on her feet. The grizzly slashed Daisy's head with claws as long as Vick's forearm, knocking her onto her back. Daisy rolled to her feet and ran toward the fountain. The grizzly chased her.

Vick realized this was their chance to run. Tara had

stopped short of him and was watching Daisy, her hands clasped in front of her like she was praying.

"Tara. We have to go!" Vick grasped her shoulders, but she spun out of his grip, not taking her eyes off Daisy, who had climbed to the top tier of the fountain, the high ground. Water pelted Daisy as the grizzly studied her from the ground. He climbed into the water, stood on his hind legs, grasped the lip of the second tier, and boosted himself up.

He was too big and awkward to reach the top tier. Like Tiny, this grizzly thing wasn't nearly as quick or graceful as Daisy. Tara was way ahead of Ms. Alba's crew when it came to body design.

Daisy glanced around, and Vick knew just what she was thinking at that moment: Is there something up here I can use as a weapon? But there was nothing—it was an empty bowl of water.

Instead, Daisy leaped, landing on the grizzly. The two of them hit the lip of the second tier and tumbled into the shallow water in the wide bottom pool. The grizzly's jaws clamped down, his teeth closing inches from Daisy's face. When he opened his mouth again, Daisy reached inside, attacking something she'd spotted in there. She pulled her arm out just as the jaws clamped down again.

An instant later Daisy was up and running toward Vick and Tara.

Vick grabbed Tara's hand. *"Run!"*

When they reached South Michigan Avenue, Vick kept going, right out into traffic. A bus screeched to a stop to avoid hitting them. Or maybe to avoid hitting Daisy, who had caught up to them.

Vick glanced back. Daisy had done something to the grizzly when she reached into its mouth—it was listing to one side, and kept trailing off at an angle from them before correcting course.

Everywhere Vick looked, people were running away.

"Help us!" Vick called to a woman watching from a second-story window.

"I called the police!" she shouted back.

Vick was pretty sure calling the police was useless. East had said Ms. Alba told the police what to do, not the other way around.

They fled down LaSalle Street. Even damaged, the four-legged grizzly closed ground quickly. Daisy dropped back, lunged, and feinted at the grizzly, trying to slow it down.

Steel claws raked the sidewalk inches short of Vick's foot as they reached the bridge.

Vick was gasping for breath by the time they made it

across. Head down, he nearly plowed into Tara, who had stopped short.

A block away, Ms. Alba was standing in front of a van parked lengthwise to block off traffic, her arms folded. Vick counted seven watchdogs spread along the street and sidewalks in front of her. Some were as big as the grizzly, others the size of raccoons.

They were surrounded.

Daisy stood on her hind legs to grip the door handle on a minivan and tore the locked door open. She looked at them pointedly. Vick scrambled into the front seat right on Tara's heels. Daisy closed the door behind Vick and turned to face the watchdogs.

At least a dozen people were watching out their windows. Others had gathered a few car lengths beyond Ms. Alba. More onlookers were arriving every second, none getting too close, no one stepping up to help. Although honestly, what could they do?

Glancing left and right, keeping her eyes on the watchdogs, Daisy reached under the minivan and tore out its muffler pipe. She climbed onto the roof as Ms. Alba's watchdogs converged around them.

The biggest watchdog now that the grizzly was trailing reminded Vick of a gorilla. It had long front legs and shorter back ones, a flat face more human than animal. It lunged for Daisy's back leg, pulling her off balance.

Daisy swung the pipe and flattened the steel gorilla's hand.

A six-legged orange thing with a head on either end, mouths full of razor teeth, leaped onto the hood of the van. One of its legs crashed through the windshield as it scrambled to get at Daisy. The pipe flashed into view, shattering one of its three eyes and knocking it backward.

The van was surrounded by watchdogs, snapping and slashing at Daisy.

Tara shrieked and clapped her hands over her eyes. A Doberman-sized watchdog was staring into her window. It was like something out of a nightmare: it had four eyes and a wide snout, and sections of its face were painted red, yellow, and blue, like some demonic clown.

It drove its face right through the window.

Vick wrapped his arms around Tara and backpedaled away from the thing. Tara was screaming; Vick's mouth was cranked open but no sound was coming out, because his chest was frozen. He wasn't even breathing. The thing kept coming, pushing its way into the van. When it opened its mouth, Vick expected to see a row of sharp metal teeth. Instead, there was a buzz saw.

The saw began to rotate; a high-pitched whining drowned out Tara's screams as the watchdog struggled to reach them. Vick pushed Tara, who'd curled up into a ball, between the seats and into the back, then scrambled after her as the blade inside the thing's mouth lunged for his leg.

The van's ceiling dented as Daisy leaped off, clearing outreached claws, and landed on the sidewalk. Vick heard the screech of steel against steel, and then the van was tipping. Vick fell toward the side window, landing on Tara as the thing trying to reach them suddenly went slack, its back end crushed between the van and the ground. Daisy had tipped the van onto it, Vick realized.

Through the rear window Vick saw Daisy on the sidewalk surrounded by watchdogs, bashing heads with the muffler pipe. Her front right paw was hanging useless, wires jutting from the wrist.

The grizzly, its face crushed, charged at Daisy, eager to get at her. Probably realizing she wasn't going to be able to hold them off, Daisy stepped on the much-slower grizzly's head and tried to vault over it, but the grizzly managed to clamp its huge jaws on her ankle. It jerked her to the pavement. Daisy reached up and slashed the grizzly's underside, disabling one of its hind legs and then the other. The grizzly's hind end crumpled, but it stubbornly clung to Daisy's leg as the others closed in.

"Daisy. Oh no. Daisy." Vick had to wrap both arms around Tara to keep her from going out to help Daisy.

Daisy reached down with her good hand and detached the leg the grizzly was clinging to. Freed, she charged unsteadily toward Ms. Alba, who was all alone in front of her white van. Watchdogs closed in on Daisy from behind.

Ms. Alba didn't run. She held her ground, arms folded, expression as serene and unreadable as ever.

When Daisy was four car lengths from her, Ms. Alba shouted a command. Dozens of white rat-sized robot bodyguards surged out of the open rear door of the van.

"Look out!" Tara screamed.

Daisy veered, trying to reach the line of stores, but without her back leg she was slow and clumsy. The tiny bodyguards swarmed up her limbs. Daisy bit the rat-things off, crushing them in her long, narrow jaws as they tore off her armored protective plates. Then the big watchdogs reached her.

They had to get out of there while the watchdogs were distracted. Vick pulled Tara toward the back door. He swung the latch and pushed it with both feet. The door dropped open.

A hundred yards away, they were tearing Daisy apart.

"Daisy—*run!*" Tara shouted. "Get away."

Vick thought she must be losing it. Daisy couldn't run—they were all over her.

A section of Daisy's lower back wriggled free and rolled to the ground. Vick squinted. None of the watchdogs had torn the piece off—it had pulled loose on its own.

The piece sprouted four legs and ran. As it leaped onto the hood of a car and dashed from roof to trunk before springing to the next parked vehicle, Vick realized what it was: Daisy. The original Daisy.

As the two-headed watchdog wrenched Big Daisy's head off her limp form, Little Daisy sprinted toward freedom.

"The chip wasn't in her head?" Vick said.

"Of course not," Tara said. "Why in the world would you put a watchdog's brain in its head? That's the first place the enemy attacks."

That was true. Still, Vick never would have thought to put a watchdog's brain in her back end.

Gesturing wildly at Little Daisy's fleeing form, Ms. Alba raced toward her watchdogs. "The little one. Get the little one."

A raccoon-sized watchdog was the first to break out of the pile and give chase. The side of its head was caved in from blows from the muffler pipe, but it still moved faster than Little Daisy.

"Run. *Run*," Tara called.

Every single watchdog gave chase. Daisy broke into the traffic on the crossing street, weaving and leaping to avoid being run over.

When Ms. Alba's pack reached the crossing street, they were met by screeching brakes and a chorus of honking horns. A taxi slammed into the two-headed model; it crumpled and went under the taxi's wheels.

The bridge across the Chicago River was just beyond the crossing street. Even from more than a block away, Vick could see the raccoon-sized watchdog rake Little Daisy to the blacktop just as she reached it. She was up again an instant later, but the much bigger watchdog pounced. Its jaws snapped closed.

Tara let out an agonized, warbling scream as Little Daisy's back half was crushed inside those steel jaws. Daisy struggled, pushing against the watchdog's cone-shaped snout with her front legs, but she couldn't break free. The watchdog swung its head, shaking her like a chew toy, then dropped her mangled body to the bridge's walkway.

Daisy didn't give up. Her back end crushed, she dragged herself with her front paws, inching toward the railing.

Ms. Alba, who had just crossed the street, cried out, "Get her!" as Daisy gripped a rusted steel crossbeam and hoisted herself over the foot rail blocking her from the water. The watchdog lunged just as Daisy, trailing severed wires, tumbled into the river.

Ms. Alba threw her fists in the air and howled in frustration.

Vick wanted to enjoy the moment, but he couldn't. Ms. Alba hadn't won, but they'd lost Daisy.

"We have to run. Now," Vick said. Ms. Alba was at the bridge railing, peering into the deep black water of the Chicago River, but Vick had no doubt she was going to set her watchdogs on them as soon as she got over the shock.

It started to rain.

Vick grasped Tara's arm and pulled her back the way they'd come. Tara dug in her heels, whimpering, not wanting to leave Daisy.

"She's gone, Tara. We have to run or we'll die." Vick wiped tears from his cheek, then tugged harder.

Something finally clicked inside Tara. She stopped resisting and started running.

A police car passed, its blue bubble flashing. Vick wondered how long the police had been watching the chaos from a distance, on Ms. Alba's orders.

CHAPTER 13

They stopped to rest in the overhang in front of a Wendy's. It was pouring. Vick was soaked down to his socks.

"Where are we going?" Tara asked.

"Back to the apartment where we slept last night."

Tara grabbed his arm. "*No*. We can't go there."

She was right. They wouldn't be safe once the rough characters squatting in that abandoned building realized Daisy wasn't there to protect them. They were back where they'd started when Mom died. Nowhere to go. No one to turn to.

"Back to the Salvation Army, then." Vick felt a surge

of dread at the thought of going back to that shelter packed with men smoking cigarettes, stealing, fighting.

Tara grabbed Vick's hand and dug her fingers in until it hurt. "That place is horrible. I don't want to go back there. Let's go back to the church. *Please.*"

Without Daisy? Torch would beat Vick to a pulp for some of the snide comments he'd made.

You want her to fart "Jingle Bells" while she works?

No, bad idea.

"We'll find somewhere new. Another roof. We can hide there until things settle down."

"*No.*" Tara let her legs drop from under her so Vick was supporting all her weight. "No. *Not another roof.*"

"We can't go back to the church. They don't want us without Daisy."

"They *do* want us. Yes, they *do.*" She dropped to the ground, her hands balled into fists and eyes squeezed shut. "They *do.*" She was going into complete meltdown mode. Vick couldn't blame her. His windpipe felt like it was closing by the second, each breath making a familiar squeal. His inhaler was in that apartment. He'd been stupid not to carry it with him at all times.

They weren't back to where they'd been when Mom died—they were much, much worse off than that. Back then they didn't have Ms. Alba to worry about. Vick leaned against the big window of the Wendy's and slid down until he was sitting next to Tara, who was screaming and thrashing. He thought he should cradle her head so she didn't hit it on the concrete, but he didn't have the strength, just didn't have the strength to reach that far. He was done. He had nothing left.

Four teenage girls came out of Wendy's. They stared at Tara. Or maybe at Vick. He looked over his shoulder and saw others inside the restaurant gawking at them.

He closed his eyes. "Please help us. *Somebody please help us.*"

One of the teenage girls set her French fries beside Vick before heading off.

The rain kept pouring down. Tara went on screaming. Vick kept his eyes closed, wanting his mom to come and take care of him. What he would give for one hug from her, a word of encouragement whispered in his ear.

The phone in his back pocket rang. Vick had forgotten about it, and suddenly realized Ms. Alba might be tracking them with it. He pulled it from his pocket; the screen immediately expanded to show Ms. Alba walking briskly, with Stripe trailing behind her, holding an umbrella over her head.

"Now you've got nothing to bargain with, nothing to protect you, and I'm angry. Good decision to turn down my offer?"

She waited for Vick to answer. He kept his mouth shut.

"I don't think so. I put a two-thousand-dollar bounty on each of you. You're both in bigger trouble than you can imagine."

She disconnected.

The street began to spin. Vick wasn't getting enough air; he felt like he was about to pass out.

A bounty?

A couple of twenty-something guys with tattoos and shaved heads came out of the restaurant. Vick dropped his chin and stared at the pavement. They had to get off the streets, find somewhere to hide.

Hands trembling, Vick snapped the phone card in half and tossed it to the ground. "Okay. We'll go to the church."

Tara went on wailing. She hadn't heard him over the noise she was making.

"We'll go to the church!" he shouted.

It was like shutting off a faucet. She stopped immediately, and then sprang up from the pavement. "North will be so happy to see me."

He probably would. The rest of them, not so much.

CHAPTER 14

Tara knocked on the door. Vick leaned against the wall, his breath coming in a tight squeal.

"Who is it?" It was Rando.

"Tara and Vick," Tara called.

There was a sharp *bang* on the door from the inside. "You've got to be kidding me. *Now* you show up? Get lost."

"Get out of the way." East's voice this time. "Move. Out of the way."

Locks clicked, bars slid free. The door opened a few inches.

"Alba put a price on your heads. Word is spreading online."

"I know. Alba called to tell me," Vick said.

The door opened wider. East took his arm. "Come on."

"*No.*" Rando got between them and blocked the door.

Torch, who was standing right behind Rando, said, "They're as good as dead. From the way he's breathing, Vick there sounds like he may beat the bounty hunters to it. You bring them in here and Alba finds out? She'll put a contract out on *us.* I'm not risking my neck because he screwed up."

"Because you never screwed up," East said.

Torch poked his own chest. "This ain't about me."

"If we turn them away, they'll last about two hours," East said. "You know that."

Torch spit on the floor, then wiped his mouth. "That's their problem."

Rando, who was still blocking the door, didn't say anything.

This was exactly what Vick had expected. Bullies— that's all they were. "East said I had you all wrong, that once I got to know you I'd see what good guys you were." It was hard to speak with his lungs so tight. "I knew Daisy was the only reason you wanted us to stay. That's why we didn't." He turned and took Tara's hand. "Come on, let's get out of here."

"Where are we going?" Tara asked.

"Just . . . let's go." Vick had no idea where to go, where

to hide. East had said they wouldn't last two hours. He believed her.

"Hang on," Rando called after them.

Vick kept walking, down the hall and into the stairwell. He had nothing more to say to Rando.

There were footsteps on the stairs behind them; when Vick reached the chapel, Rando fell into step beside him.

"I'm not saying you're right about everything you just said, but maybe you have a point."

Vick wanted to pick up his pace and leave Rando behind, but he couldn't walk any faster. He could barely breathe.

"You can crash for a couple of days if you want."

Tara slowed. "You hear that? We can stay."

"*No, they can't.*" Torch was following a few paces behind them. East and North were behind Torch. It was sort of like a parade, only lamer, and no one was smiling.

"East is right," Rando said. "If we turn them away, we might as well shoot them ourselves. I don't want that on my head."

"You take them in and you won't *have* a head."

Vick pulled Tara along, steering her toward the big double doors that led to the street. He could hear the rain outside. It sounded like applause.

Rando grabbed Vick's shoulder and twisted him around so they were facing each other. He narrowed his eyes. "If you go out there, your sister's as good as dead. Don't be an idiot."

"That's just what I was thinking," Tara said. "Vick, don't be an idiot."

It was hard to think straight when he couldn't breathe. There was no getting around it: he was having a full-blown asthma attack. He squeezed his eyes shut and tried to focus.

He kept seeing Daisy, dragging her front end off that bridge. It was like he'd lost another family member.

Tara pried her hand loose from his. "Well, I'm staying. If you don't want to, fine."

"If they stay, I go," Torch said. "And I take my equipment with me."

Rando turned to Torch. "Come on, man, don't be a ratbag."

The words seemed to take some of the air out of Torch. He turned his head, spit, and then raised his gaze to give Vick a withering look. "If anything happens to either of my friends because of this, I'll collect the bounty myself."

They paraded back to the basement, this time with East leading the way. She looked at her phone as she walked. "Alba has fifty people dragging the river. They have nets across it every couple of blocks."

That meant they hadn't found Daisy. Not yet, anyway.

North fell into step beside Tara. "I'm sorry Daisy died. I cried when I heard."

"Thanks. She liked you a lot."

In the basement, East sank into the mattress beside little North. "*Now.* Tell us how Daisy could do all those amazing things."

"I'll tell you." Tara looked at Vick. "I found the chip, so I get to tell them."

Vick shrugged. Evidently Tara thought telling them was some sort of special treat. He sat on the floor and leaned up against the wall, trying to breathe.

"I found this chip in the dump—a special chip, like nothing I've ever seen. I checked out the programming on my handheld and even *I* couldn't follow it."

"That's why Alba was searching the dump," Vick added.

"How did *Alba's* crew make something like that?" Rando asked.

"They didn't, dummy," Tara said. "If they made it, they wouldn't want it back so bad, because they could just make more."

"So they *stole* it," East said. "They were going to reverse-engineer it and make more, only someone accidentally tossed it in the trash."

"Who'd they steal it *from*?" Rando asked. "It had to be some major tech company."

Vick had been trying to figure out what that chip was since he found out about it. Daisy had been like no other robot he'd ever seen. The chip was something very new.

"I know exactly what it is." Torch tapped on his phone.

"Do you?" East sounded skeptical, or maybe just annoyed because Torch had made such a big deal about Vick and Tara staying. "Why don't you fill us in there, Sherlock?"

Torch expanded his screen so they could all see. It was a discussion thread on a website called *Military Tech Underground*. The heading was "Military Testing New AI Soldier."

"If you're in the business of building weapons, it helps to keep tabs on what the big boys are up to." Torch tapped his temple. "Gives you new ideas."

He read the discussion thread out loud, stumbling on some of the bigger words. The military had been using robot soldiers for a decade, but they had to be embedded in human platoons, because like all robots, they were stupid. There were rumors that a new generation of artificial soldiers was being tested. They could carry out missions independently. Vick tried to imagine an entire platoon of robots. Robots led by other robots. It was a scary thought.

"So Daisy was a soldier." Tara choked up and started

to cry again. Vick choked back tears of his own. There was no way he was going to cry in front of these guys.

"That's why she was such a good fighter," Torch said. "That's what she was programmed to do. Plus repair herself, if she got damaged in the field."

So now they had a good guess about where Daisy came from. What good was that? She was gone.

A wave of despair rolled over Vick. How were they going to survive this? They couldn't hide in this basement forever, and as soon as they showed their faces on the street, they were dead. He felt like he was breathing through a straw. He needed his inhaler.

He looked at East. "I have to go to the place where we stayed last night. There's medicine there I need."

"Yeah, you don't sound so good," East said.

Rando stood. "I'll get it. Where is this place?"

Vick started to answer, and realized he didn't really know. He thought he could walk to the neighborhood and maybe the right street, but he hadn't paid attention to where the building was, because Daisy knew, and she was always with them. "I don't know. I'd know it if I saw it. I guess I have to go myself."

"I'll go with you." Rando grabbed a ratty gray jacket with a hood and tossed it to Vick. "Put this on and keep your head down. Hopefully no one will recognize you in the dark."

They walked the first few blocks in silence. It was hard for Vick to talk, plus he didn't have anything to say to Rando.

Rando finally broke the silence. "You still pissed off about the fire escape?"

"I just—" He paused to take a wheezing breath. "Like to keep to myself. I appreciate you letting us stay and everything." Walking was making it even harder to catch his breath. "I just feel more comfortable. Being on my own."

Rando nodded. "I can respect that."

They went back to walking in silence, but Vick felt like he needed to say something. Rando had made an effort, now it was on Vick.

"Where'd you learn to make watchdogs?"

Rando looked up at the night sky, as if the answer was written in the stars. "Mercy Home for Boys and Girls. Vocational training in robotics repair. They wanted you to have a way to make a living when you left."

"When did you leave?"

Rando turned his head to spit into a puddle. "Eleven. The city cut the funding. One Friday the lady in charge called an assembly and told us we could stay if we wanted, but the power was gonna be cut on Saturday, and it wasn't coming back. And neither was she."

"Seems like we all got kicked out of somewhere. East's own parents kicked her out."

"Is that what she told you?" Rando asked.

The words startled Vick. "Yeah. Why?"

"Nothing." Rando pointed his flashlight. "Do any of these buildings look familiar?"

In the third tenement building they tried, Vick recognized an empty, torn-open suitcase they'd had to step around to climb the stairs. "This is it."

They hurried to the third floor, tossed Vick and Tara's stuff into their backpacks sitting empty by the door, and were out of the apartment in less than five minutes.

On the staircase, Vick took a hit from his inhaler. Almost immediately, his chest loosened and his windpipe relaxed. He should have asked Daisy to get him more medicine, instead of taking a ride on the Ferris wheel.

Rando, who was ahead of Vick, stopped halfway down the last flight of stairs.

A guy was standing at the bottom holding a length of rope. He was in his twenties, with a long ponytail poking through the back of a Cubs cap.

Vick's throat closed right back up.

"I'm gonna need you to move clear, Rando," the guy said.

Rando stayed where he was. "You're really taking Alba's side in this, Pete?"

"I'm not taking anyone's side. You want to pay me

twenty-one hundred to walk away, I'm happy to do business with you."

"You know I don't got twenty-one hundred dollars."

"That's why you need to move clear."

Vick wanted to turn and run as fast as he could back up the stairs. He knew that was a bad idea, that he was safer staying close to Rando, but it was hard to stand there.

"Alba ain't from around here," Rando said. "She's from California, or Florida, or some place like that. She comes walking into our neighborhood and wants to take over, and what are you going to do about it? Help her?"

"I'm done talking, Rando. You better stand clear."

Rando talked faster. "Don't try to act like it's all just business, like one side's as good as another, because you know that ain't how it is. This kid took on Alba right out in the street in broad daylight—I know you heard about that—and he hurt her bad, which is more than either of us can say. He's a hero. He's the good guy. You really want to hurt the good guy?" He pointed at Pete. "You know what that makes you, if you hurt the good guy? It makes you the bad guy."

Pete lowered his gaze a few inches, and then wiped his mouth.

"Don't take her blood money," Rando said.

Pete cursed. "He's already dead. You know that, right? It's just gonna be someone else who gets him."

"They can't get him if he's not here."

"You better hurry up and get them on a bus."

"Thanks, Pete. I owe you one."

"Yeah, yeah. Some fourteen-year-old punk owes me one. Lucky me." Pete pushed the front door open and disappeared.

Vick sat on the stairs, his legs rubbery.

Rando sat a few steps below Vick. He burst out laughing. "I can't believe I talked him out of it."

"I can't believe you tried."

Still chuckling with relief, Rando said, "My heart was going like crazy."

"I don't get it. Why didn't you just move out of the way and let him have me?"

Surprised, Rando spun to look at Vick. "What would I have told your sister when I got back?"

Vick didn't know what to say. It had been a long time since anyone stood up for him, and the last person in the world he expected to was Rando. Well, except for Torch.

Rando stood and ran his hand over his shaved head. "Let's get out of here before he changes his mind."

"Yeah." Vick stood, his legs still shaking. "Thanks. Thanks for saving my life."

"Yeah." Rando said it like it was no big thing.

CHAPTER 15

Vick checked on Tara, who was sitting in a pew, her head on her knees, her arms wrapped around her head. He went and sat beside her.

"I miss her so much," Tara said.

Vick put his arm across her shoulders as she started to cry again. "Me too." He pictured Daisy loping around this chapel with North on her back, like she was a steel pony. She'd only been a machine—Vick knew that—but losing her hurt worse than he ever would have imagined. It wasn't just that Daisy had been their protector. She'd been *smart*, like a person. She'd known what was going on.

He watched North run along the balcony of the chapel, disappearing behind blue rafters, reappearing in front of cracked and broken stained-glass windows, laughing as if he didn't have a care in the world. Vick worried that the balcony wasn't stable, that North might get hurt. It was still safer than playing outside, though.

Speaking of which, someone had left one of the big front doors open a crack. Anyone walking by could spot them through that crack.

Vick pushed himself to his feet. "Be right back."

Rando must have left it open when he went to buy food from the convenience store. Vick could picture him trying to kick it closed with his hands full of bags, and not quite making it.

Ever since Rando stood between Vick and that guy with the rope three days ago, Vick had been trying to figure him out. He'd laughed while scaring a crying girl, then risked his life to save a kid he barely knew. All Vick could think was, Torch had been the one banging on the fire escape, and Rando laughed along because sometimes you just went along with your friends even if you didn't agree with what they were doing.

Vick slowed as he approached the open door. There was something on the ground, jammed in the doorway. Vick thought it was a brick, or a piece of trash, but as he got closer he saw it was caked in dried and cracking mud. And it was moving. It was trying to claw its way through the door.

It had to be a rat, Vick realized, disgusted. He took a step back as the door creaked open another inch and the thing dragged itself inside, claws digging into the filthy tile floor.

Vick studied the thing's mangled back half. It was no rat. *"Tara."*

He stood frozen, afraid that if he moved he'd see it was just a rat after all, that his wishful thinking had created an illusion.

Tara stood up from her pew. "What?"

Vick pointed across the vestibule, where a mangled, mud-covered Daisy was dragging herself toward them.

Tara shrieked. She raced to Daisy, lifted her gently, and carried her broken body in cupped hands. "She's alive," she breathed.

CHAPTER 16

Everyone huddled around Tara, staring down at the front half of Daisy.

"How did she know to come here?" Rando asked.

"She wasn't going to climb three flights of stairs," Tara said. "She must have thought if she made it here, you'd know how to reach us." Tara ran her finger along the top of Daisy's head, petting her like she was a miniature puppy dog. "You're so smart."

Vick had almost forgotten just how smart she was. He was so glad to see her.

"I still can't believe you hid your watchdog's brain in her butt," Torch said, snickering.

"We should get moving," Rando said. "We've got work to do."

No one had said it out loud, but they all knew what they needed to do now: build Daisy a new watchdog body.

"Where are we going to get parts?" Vick asked. They'd used the best of the parts on the roof to make the first Daisy watchdog.

"You're going to steal them," Rando said, staring right at Vick, daring him to disagree. "You, East, and Torch."

Vick started to argue, but Rando spoke over him. "Because you're good at locating the right parts, but you suck at building watchdogs. Is that about right?"

All Vick could do was nod.

"Then get going."

"What about the dump?" Vick asked.

Rando looked annoyed. "No junk parts. Alba's army tore her apart once, and I'm still not sure how we're going to keep them from doing it again, but for starters we can make her as big and bad as possible."

"Wait, what about the bounty on me?"

Torch grabbed his sleeve and tugged. "I got that covered. Come on."

■ ■ ■

Vick studied his new look in the bathroom's broken mirror. One side of his head was bald, the hair on the other side bright red. Even with the sleeves cut off, Torch's purple Ghost Rider T-shirt just about swallowed him.

Torch looked pleased. "No one's going to recognize your punk face now."

That was true, and Vick would rather look bad than be dead. He went downstairs to find Tara. If he was going to locate the right parts, he needed to know what Tara had in mind for Daisy the Third.

When Tara saw him, she clapped her hand over her mouth. Her shoulders bounced with silent laughter. "Mom's going to kill you."

The comment wiped the smirks off both their faces.

"She would, wouldn't she?" Vick said. He tried to shake off the sadness. "What do you need me to get for the new Daisy?"

"Argon-injected clamp. Her jaws are going to work like a bear trap." She clapped her hands together to demonstrate. "Magnesium alloy teeth, so the tips don't bend when she bites down on something hard."

Argon-injected clamp? Vick had no idea what that was, let alone where to find it. And he only knew what magnesium alloy was because . . .

Because the barbershop robots that replaced Mom

had magnesium alloy scissors and clippers built onto the ends of their limbs. Guaranteed to stay sharp for fifty years. Vick broke into a grin. Now, *there* was a robot he would love to hack up for parts.

"Who needs a haircut?" he called.

CHAPTER 17

At three a.m., Versacci's Beauty Spa was deserted. They'd counted on that—who would want a haircut at three a.m.? Two shiny silver salon bots stood at attention by their chairs, each with a clean, neatly folded barber smock across one arm. They had four arms, an attractive but basic metal face that could make about three expressions, and wheeled bottom halves. What use did they have for legs, since they never left the smooth floor of the barbershop?

Vick eyed the bot at the farther chair. That had been Mom's station for eleven years. If it was still hers, she'd still be alive.

"Can I help you?" the bot closest to the door asked,

smiling brightly. The smile was so bright it made the bot look a little deranged.

Torch was waving through a 3-D catalog that showed how he would look sporting different hairdos, an aluminum bat clutched in his other hand. Vick ignored the station by the wall opposite the far chair, where images of him with various haircuts had materialized as soon as he walked through the door.

"Yeah, I think I want this one." Torch pointed at an image of himself with long, golden locks like the Mighty Thor.

"Sure, I can help you with that." The robot unfolded the smock with a crisp snap. "Have a seat. How about that Cubs game? Are you a baseball fan?"

Torch stayed where he was. "No."

"How about movies? Have you seen *One Blue Two White*?"

"Nope." Torch folded his arms.

"How about that Dow Jones Industrial Average? Are you an investor?"

"I'm *fourteen*. What do you think?"

The bot switched from that big, crazy smile to a frown. "Do you want to tell me your problems?"

"I don't have any problems. My life is just peachy. Couldn't be better."

The bot's mouth flattened into a thin, straight line. "Gardening? Popular music? Current events?"

"Uh-uh." Torch slapped the bat with his palm.

"I'm afraid that's the extent of my conversational repertoire. I can still cut your hair, though." It patted the back of the barber chair.

Torch swung the bat. He nailed the bot in the side of the head. Sparks shot from its eyes as it toppled.

This got the attention of the other bot. It raised its scissor arm. "I am legally authorized to defend the property of Versacci's Beauty Spa from vandalism or theft. These scissors are razor-sharp, and can be lethal if—"

Torch wound up and whacked that bot, too, knocking it to the ground. "Yeah, see, the problem with that is, you're on wheels."

Vick unslung his backpack, and then pulled out the laser cutter Rando had given him. East was already standing on the wrist of the bot's scissor hand, pinning it to the floor. Vick hurried over and sliced the hand off with the laser cutter.

Then he went to work on the rest of the bot, starting with the arm.

"I'm recording this. Every bit of it," the bot said.

Vick set aside the severed arm. "That would be a real problem, if we were going to leave your head behind, or if barber bots could send messages. But who's going to spend money connecting a barber bot to the Internet?"

He sliced off another arm, leaving a gouge in the white floor.

"A microscopic tracer chip was inserted into me by my manufacturer. No matter where you take me—"

"Roll it over," East said.

Vick rolled it over. East ran the chip-deactivating wand over its spine.

"If only you had one to deactivate its mouth."

"Here. Give me that." East held out her hand.

Vick handed her the cutter. She sliced across the bot's neck.

"Wait," the bot said. "Please, don't do that. There's a great deal of complex circuitry between my head and torso. If you sever my head—"

The bot's eyes went blank as the head dropped to the floor with a leaden *thunk*.

"Oh, man. I was looking forward to that part," Vick said.

Torch grinned at him. "So there is a little mean streak in you after all. I was starting to wonder."

"When it comes to these bots, I'm nothing but mean streak. That bot took my mom's job."

Torch glanced up at him, surprised. He pointed at the bot's head. "This one right here?"

"That one."

Torch nodded. "Which is why you picked this salon. I get it."

Vick finished cutting the bot up, then stuffed the pieces they could use into the big, roomy backpack Rando had also supplied.

"We all set?" East asked, hefting her backpack, which was stuffed with pieces from the other bot.

"Let's go."

They headed for the door.

▶

The pack got heavy in a hurry. Vick struggled to keep up as they crossed Ashland Avenue at a brisk walk. He'd expected to run all the way home, but East explained that running drew unwanted attention.

"We still haven't figured out how one watchdog is going to beat an army," Torch said as they walked. "As soon as Alba sees Daisy in action, she's going to figure out what happened, and this time she's going to send everything she's got after her."

Vick didn't have an answer. All he could think was for Daisy to get them out of Chicago to somewhere safer. But where would they be safe, with a contract on their heads? Ms. Alba could spread their photos and her bounty offer to gangs and criminals all over the country using the Net. All over the world, if she wanted. If they gave her the chip, he could only think that she'd kill them, and if they didn't, she'd probably kill them, too. Daisy gave them some protection, but Ms. Alba had an army of watchdogs, and an army of thugs. The only way they'd be safe was to beat her, but they'd need an army of their own to do that.

"An army," Vick said out loud.

East, who was a few paces ahead, glanced back. "What?"

They needed an army. "Daisy's a soldier. She was designed to be part of an army, to lead other bots."

"So?" East said.

"Let's build her an army."

Torch stopped walking. His mouth open, breathing hard, he grabbed Vick's shoulder and shook it roughly. "You mean, just keep building them. Stop Alba for good."

Vick nodded.

"Wow," East said. "That's a gutsy idea."

When they got back to the church, Tara had cleaned up Little Daisy and rebuilt her back end. As they began unloading the parts from the salon bots, Tara jumped up and down, clapping her hands. She'd never had shiny *or* new parts to work with before.

Little North, eager to help, took an arm from Vick and carried it to the table.

"The scissors are magnesium alloy," Vick said.

"Teeth." Tara tapped one of the scissors.

"Now, what's an argon-injected clamp, and where do we find one?" Vick asked.

East pulled out her phone and tapped on it awhile. "They're in big air-conditioning units. Any made in the past ten years, anyway."

"Piece of cake," Torch said. "Shoot me some specs. I can handle that one myself."

Vick turned back to Tara and Rando. "What else?"

CHAPTER 18

"Okay, confession time," East said as they left the church. "You know how I said I grew up a few blocks from here?"

"Yeah?"

"I didn't. I'm from the suburbs. Naperville."

"Naperville?" That was a surprise. East seemed like the model Chicago city girl—tough, street-smart, someone who would have zero interest in makeup and heels, even if she could afford them. She did not seem like a Naperville girl. Naperville was an upscale suburb.

"Yup. Soccer every Saturday, neighborhood swim team in the summer, the whole deal. Rando knows, but Torch doesn't. And don't tell him."

"Don't worry." So that's what Rando had meant when he'd said *Is that what she told you?*

"Why do you tell people you're from the city?"

"If people know you're from the suburbs, they think they can take advantage of you. They think everyone out there is too green to cross the street without a GPS and their momma."

Vick had to admit, that was how he thought of Naperville kids. Although deep down, he'd always felt he was meant to be a suburb kid. He'd lived in the suburbs until his dad took off when Vick was six.

"Did your parents really kick you and North out of the house?"

East gave him a sheepish look. "I tell people that to build my street cred. Mom died right after North was born. Dad lost it a few years ago, started dressing in sheets and claiming he was a king from the lost city of Atlantis. Social services took us away from him, and we ran away from social services." They paused at the corner to let a car pass. "I want you to know the truth, since it looks like we're going to be friends after all."

Friends seemed like the wrong word. You played video games with friends, you didn't fight to stay alive. Vick couldn't think of a better word for what they were becoming. All he knew was, it was a whole lot more than friends.

▶

East peered around the corner, then quickly pulled back and pressed up against the brick wall beside Vick.

"Here it comes," she whispered.

Vick felt so strange, lurking in a dark alley like some thug getting ready to mug someone. The domestic bot passed the alley where they were hiding, oblivious, pulling a wheeled cart filled with grocery bags. East sprang off the wall and strode to catch up, with Vick right behind, each of them holding one end of a rope.

East looped the rope around the front of the bot.

"What—" the robot managed before East and Vick tugged it off its feet. It was one of those cutesy retro models, not equipped for self-defense against anything bigger than a badger, so there was no need for Vick to do anything more than step on its chest while East went to work with the laser cutter.

"What are you doing?" the bot asked, its head lifted so it could study the laser cutter that was shearing its leg off at the hip.

"We're stealing you. We're going to use your parts to make a watchdog to protect us from sort of a corporate warlord," Vick said.

"Oh dear, no! You can't do that. My owner could never get along without me." It struggled futilely as East tugged the leg free and handed it to Vick. "Stop that. Give that back."

"I don't think so." Vick stuffed the leg in his pack. It was hard to feel guilty for cutting robots apart. They were such morons.

▶

The door swung open just as they reached it.

"Come see!" Grinning, North grabbed Vick's hand and pulled him inside.

As Vick stepped into the basement, he found himself breathless. Daisy was testing her new legs, lifting them one at a time, bending each joint.

She was magnificent. She was terrifying.

The body was vaguely wolflike like the old Daisy, but all smooth, shining silver, her snout wider and gleaming with sharp teeth like the big bad wolf in some nightmare fairy tale. Even on all fours, she was taller at the shoulder than Vick. Her front paws had two well-defined, two-jointed fingers and an opposable thumb. She'd be able to grip things with ease.

"Nice," Vick said.

Rando set down a mini-blowtorch and rubbed his eyes. "Your sister here is incredible. She improvises new designs on the fly like they're nothing. The new Daisy has three-hundred-sixty-degree vision, she can climb a little, and those jaws can bite through anything."

"Now, don't you feel bad about all the times you were mean to me?" Tara patted Daisy's head. "She's ready. How many more watchdogs do we need?"

"As many as we can make," East said.

CHAPTER 19

"I need something round." Tara, who was bent over a half-finished watchdog that resembled a giant red ant, traced a circle in the air with her finger, her gaze a thousand miles away.

"Yeah, I know what round is," Rando said. "You think you can be a little more specific?"

Vick turned away, laughing. It was nice to let someone else be Tara's assistant for a change. He surveyed the basement, which was getting crowded. A menagerie of watchdogs milled around among discarded parts and trash from food Daisy had stolen for them.

Vick's favorite was an eight-legged spider-thing that was nothing but legs and a wide, fang-filled mouth.

There was also something that resembled a six-legged crocodile, a blue-green dragon that shot fire from its mouth thanks to a gas tank you filled through a port in its side, and a huge, huge dark gray hippo-beast that just barely fit through the door. The other four watchdogs were nearly identical: wolves. A pack of wolves. Tara said they were easy to make.

Eight watchdogs and Daisy wasn't enough to take on Ms. Alba's army, but it was a start. The plan was to build thirty, then have Daisy lead her platoon to Ms. Alba's factory, where they would destroy all her watchdogs in a surprise attack.

"Hey, guys?" Dishes and silverware clinked and rattled as East fished them out of the water tub. "Just because I'm a girl doesn't mean I'm going to wash your dishes."

Vick inhaled to say he washed his and Tara's dishes every time, but changed his mind. East could probably guess who the slobs were.

The sound of those dishes clattering had caused a tug of longing in Vick's gut, and it took him a minute to realize why. Whenever Mom was angry, she'd bang pots and dishes around, purposely pulling the bottom dish from a stack to make as much noise as possible. There were a lot of little things that never failed to remind Vick of his mom, like Big Red gum, which was the only kind she ever chewed, and anything related to martial arts.

A door banged in the hallway. Everyone was suddenly on their feet.

"Where did that come from?" Torch asked.

"Upstairs, I think," Vick said.

"Definitely upstairs," Tara agreed.

East had her hand on the doorknob. "Everyone quiet." The door squealed as she opened it a few inches.

Vick could hear a man's voice, but it was too far away to make out what he was saying.

Another door banged. Whoever it was, it sounded like he was searching the church.

"Unless they have bots with them, they're in for a surprise," Rando said.

"We should get out of here, though," East said. "If they do have bots, we don't want to get pinned down with only one way in or out."

Vick turned to Daisy. "Get us out of here."

Daisy nodded.

The spider eased the door open and slipped out, responding to a wireless command sent from Daisy. All the watchdogs were linked by a closed communication system.

The spider was back in less than a minute, conveying

what it had seen to Daisy. Daisy led the other watchdogs into the hallway. A few took off in different directions, while the rest spread out around Vick and his companions, who followed right behind Daisy.

She took them up a different stairway than the one they typically used, climbing three flights instead of two so they emerged onto the balcony overlooking the chapel floor.

Daisy turned and held up one paw, her gesture clear: *Stay here.*

There were voices in the chapel.

"This place gives me the creeps." Vick immediately recognized Dixie's twangy voice and the unmistakable clacking of watchdogs prowling below. He slipped farther back from the main floor, to a broken stained-glass window that looked out over the church entrance.

What he saw out the window drained all the hope and optimism that had been building for the past week. Ms. Alba had brought an army. Watchdogs paced. White-haired thugs watched from behind parked vans and from the windows and roof across the street. As usual, the police were nowhere in sight.

Vick touched East's and Rando's shoulders to get their attention, then motioned to the window. They crept over to look.

They were in trouble. It was nine watchdogs against dozens.

Movement on the wall beyond the altar drew Vick's attention. It was their spider, climbing silently. It kept going until it was clinging to the ceiling, forty feet above the chapel floor.

Vick ventured a peek over the railing to the floor below. Besides Dixie, there were five watchdogs in view, including their old friend Tiny, good as new.

Stripe's voice broke the silence. "I found where they've been staying, but it's deserted."

"They could have gone out," Dixie said. "Send the messenger out to tell Ms. Alba—"

There was a crash, then a screech, like furniture dragging across a floor. Vick and the others leaned forward to watch as one of the pews slid into view, pushed by Daisy. She drove the wide, flat side of the pew right into Tiny, knocking him off his feet. Shouts rang out as Daisy kept going, driving Tiny across the chapel and slamming him against the wall. Daisy kept driving with her legs as Tara's metal hippo galloped into view, moving slowly, steadily gaining speed. It barreled straight at the pew and, turning at the last second, slammed into it with one steel shoulder.

Vick could hear the *crunch* from the balcony. Daisy

and the hippo let the pew fall away; Tiny fell with it, his body split, electronic innards spilling out.

They turned to face a tank on legs that was every bit as large as the hippo, a four-legged thing covered in steel spines like a porcupine, and four three-legged steel dinosaurs. Stripe and Dixie were gone. Vick hadn't seen them go, but he wasn't surprised.

The spider dropped from the ceiling, flipping upright on the way down and landing on the headless tank on legs. Using that huge mouth, the spider tore the corner of the thing open. The tank spun, trying to fling the spider off, but the spider had dug the sharp tips of its legs into the tank.

"Fire!" East shouted.

Smoke poured in through the front doors. Vick could see flames licking the stained-glass windows he'd scouted from minutes earlier. Tara clutched Vick so hard it hurt, and buried her head in his chest. "I don't like this."

They were trapped. If they went outside, Ms. Alba's army would be waiting. They couldn't even go to the ground floor without Ms. Alba's watchdogs coming after them.

Daisy's wolves had formed a circle around the three-legged dinosaurs. The dinosaurs lunged at the wolves, snapping, but the wolves stayed out of range of their big jaws.

The fire was inside the church now; it was climbing the front wall. At the other end of the chapel the altar was burning. Ms. Alba's people had set fire to both the front and back exits.

Daisy stepped between two wolves and bit a dinosaur's head clean off with one snap of her jaws. The thing's body stayed upright until one of the other dinosaurs bumped into it and knocked it clattering to the tile floor. An instant later, that dinosaur's head was gone as well.

Tara was making a high-pitched keening sound and rocking against Vick, her eyes squeezed shut. She was heading toward a meltdown.

Vick took Tara's hands in his and stared into her face. "You can't do this now, Tara. I need you to stay with me. You have to put it off, the way you did in the garbage dump, when Tiny had us trapped."

Tara opened her eyes and looked to Vick's right. She stopped making the sound. "I'll try. I'll try my best."

Coughing, East grabbed Vick's elbow and pulled him toward the stairs to the ground floor. Vick's eyes were burning from the thick smoke in the air. Rando was carrying North.

Near the front doors, a flaming rafter dropped to the floor, spitting smoke.

"They'll attack as soon as we step through the doors," Torch said.

Daisy gave Vick and Tara a hard shove toward the door. She did the same to Torch. Vick followed Daisy's direction and headed for the front doors. He had no idea what she had in mind, but she was a soldier. She knew what she was doing. Vick's lungs were burning; the air was black and red-hot.

The hippo stepped in front of them just as they reached the door. Daisy nudged Vick toward the hippo, indicating they should stay close behind it. Vick understood: it was going to act as a moving shield.

"Ready?" Vick squeezed Tara's hand.

"I don't like this." She was holding it together, though. She was controlling her meltdown, staving it off.

"Hang on. As soon as we're through this, we'll both have a good meltdown," Vick said.

Three of Ms. Alba's watchdogs crashed through the stained-glass windows at the front of the church just as Daisy rose onto her back legs and knocked the door down.

CHAPTER 20

The hippo thundered outside, trampling a pair of snapping raccoon-sized watchdogs. As soon as they were clear of the church, their little army formed a circle around Vick, Tara, and their friends. They angled to the right, directly at a pack of four or five of Ms. Alba's watchdogs.

As they drew close, the circle rotated so Tara's dragon faced Ms. Alba's charging watchdogs. A plume of fire burst from the dragon's mouth, engulfing the cluster of watchdogs. When the flame cut off, they were smoking and motionless, their inner circuitry fried. Daisy's phalanx plowed through them and kept going.

It took Ms. Alba's army a few precious seconds to re-
act, giving Daisy time to lead hers around the corner.
Wide-eyed little North was on Rando's back, clinging to
him for all he was worth.

Some of Ms. Alba's faster watchdogs caught up before they'd made it half a block. Vick spotted their friend
the grizzly toward the front of the pack, its head all fixed
up. The dragon, who was now defending the rear, held
them off with bursts of flame. There was no way they
were going to outrun Ms. Alba's army.

There was a sacrifice zone one block to their right—
nothing but piles of rubble, semidemolished buildings,
walls, and trash.

"Daisy." Vick pointed it out. "What about in there?"
It seemed like a good place to make a stand if you were
outnumbered.

Daisy studied the apocalyptic landscape for a moment, then changed direction, leading them toward it.
They skirted a towering mound of concrete, brick, and
twisted steel around a partially collapsed wall. Beyond
was more of the same—a maze of walls and twisted gird-
ers, some of it in piles, some still standing.

Daisy slowed. Her pathetically small army melted
away into the maze of ruins. Ms. Alba's people wouldn't
be able to sneak up from behind, and would have no
idea where they were.

Daisy found an office building rising out of a hill of rubble, the first few floors intact and the two outer walls peeled away. She hurried them up a stairwell to the third floor and left them there.

When she reached solid ground, Daisy grabbed a stop sign and ripped it out of the ground. She tore off the sign, which left her with a steel pole with one ragged end.

A silver six-legged beetle watchdog with huge pincers came around the corner. Daisy raced at it on three legs, clutching the pole. She drove the pole right through the beetle, skewering it. When the thing stopped moving, she yanked the pole out and moved on, heading toward the back of the building that Vick and the others were hiding in.

"I bet all of them have built-in cameras," Rando said. "That one was probably a scout, to see what it looks like in here. Alba's going to direct them."

Peering from behind a huge chunk of concrete, Vick could see Ms. Alba beyond the partially collapsed wall. She was huddled with Stripe and Dixie, talking. Dixie pointed at something in the sacrifice zone and Stripe nodded. They were planning their attack. Daisy had set things up so this really was like a battle in a war. They were outnumbered, but they had a real soldier on their side.

Vick started counting Ms. Alba's watchdogs.

"Forty," Tara said before he could finish. "There are forty."

Against nine. Even for Daisy, that seemed like too many. He watched them move around. Some of the models looked familiar, but there were new ones out there as well.

Tara sat on the floor. "She'll stop them."

"I know she will." Vick's lips felt numb as he watched those killing machines split up into groups of five. Forty divided by five equaled eight—a gang of five to go after nearly all of their watchdogs.

Vick looked around. "Does anyone see Daisy?"

"She's over there." Torch pointed her out. She was climbing a hill of rubble directly behind their hiding place, still carrying the pole. "You always want the high ground, especially in hand-to-hand combat."

"*Daisy*," Vick called.

She stopped and looked at Vick.

"There are eight groups of five. Forty total."

Daisy raised a paw to show she understood. Only three of her allies were visible from Vick's vantage point: the spider, clinging to the wall of a nearby building, and two wolves perched on a concrete slab halfway up the hill.

Five of Ms. Alba's watchdogs appeared in the gap between the wall and the mountain of debris. A second group followed right behind, heading in a different direction.

Daisy made no attempt to hide her location. The first group headed right for her. They spread out, and then picked their way up the hill of twisted steel and concrete. A sleek white model that looked a little like a panther was the first to draw close. Daisy shoved the pole through its open mouth and out the back of its head. The panther tumbled down the hill.

"Thirty-nine," Tara said.

The remaining four stopped climbing toward Daisy. They changed direction, heading toward the pair of wolves perched nearby.

"That must be Alba. She's directing them wirelessly," East said. "She saw that Daisy's plan was to pick them off one at a time. She's not going to let her do that."

Two more platoons of watchdogs surged through the gap and immediately headed up the mound of debris toward the wolves. Some of the new watchdogs were simple designs that didn't look like anything living— they were just snapping jaws on legs or, in one case, a half-dozen buzz saws on legs.

"They're going to tear those wolves apart," Torch said as more than a dozen watchdogs closed in.

A long plume of flames erupted from a gap between two slabs of concrete to the right of the wolves and lower down. Three watchdogs were engulfed in the flames, and a fourth, the walking buzz saw, was partially hit as well. Tara's dragon sprang from the gap and clambered up to join the wolves.

"Thirty-six. Thirty-six," Tara chanted, punching the air.

The watchdogs that had been closing in on the wolves stopped climbing as the dragon turned its face this way and that, threatening to toast anything that came within range.

A commotion began down to their left. Tara's metal hippo was surrounded, its back to the wall. It was too big and heavy to climb to higher ground.

As watchdogs closed in, the hippo charged the smallest in the semicircle—a thing that was all razor-sharp snapping teeth. The hippo trampled it, leaving scrap metal in its wake, but that slowed it enough for the other watchdogs to catch up.

The grizzly was part of that group. It clamped its jaws onto the hippo's hind leg at the knee and dug in with all four limbs, dragging the hippo to a stop.

The other four watchdogs swarmed. A wolf leaped at the hippo, knocking her off her feet. A squat, armored thing with a huge clubbed tail was waiting. It swung its tail in a wide arc and slammed it down on the hippo with incredible force.

The pack of watchdogs raced off, leaving the hippo motionless.

"Thirty-five," Tara whispered, her voice shaking.

Vick wrapped his arm around his sister. He knew these watchdogs were more than just robots to her. She put her whole heart into building them, and loved each one of them.

"Oh no." East pointed below the pair of wolves and the dragon. Ms. Alba's gorilla was carrying a huge rusted steel plate it must have pulled out of the wreckage. It was rectangular, at least twelve feet wide. The other watchdogs got behind the steel plate as the gorilla carried it toward the plateau.

As they drew close, the dragon blasted them with a jet of flame, but Ms. Alba's watchdogs were shielded from the worst of it.

Vick spotted movement out of the corner of his eye. Daisy was charging across the mound of debris, closing in to attack the group from behind.

She reached the rear of the group and drove the pole through a velociraptor's chest. In one fluid motion she withdrew the pole and rammed the other end into a six-legged thing's head. She towered over the other watchdogs, like an adult fighting a bunch of children.

Daisy tore through Ms. Alba's troops, while above, one of Daisy's wolves jumped from its perch, slamming into the steel plate and knocking the gorilla down the hill into the watchdogs below it.

"Thirty-one. Thirty. Twenty-nine," Tara chanted under her breath. "Look out, *look out!*"

The grizzly had loped up the hill from the opposite side of the slope. It leaped onto the cement plateau and slashed at the dragon with its powerful front paw, knocking the dragon off.

The remaining wolf closed with the grizzly, but the grizzly was twice its size. It buffeted the wolf's head like a boxer, denting it on both sides with clanging blows. The wolf managed to clamp its teeth on one of the grizzly's paws. It held on stubbornly, tugging the grizzly toward the edge of the platform as the grizzly went on pounding it with the other paw. Wolf and grizzly tumbled over the edge together. The wolf fell backward, landing right on a jutting steel beam. It rolled off and tried to stand, but its back was bent into a V, its hind legs frozen.

The battle was a chaos of moving steel, flashing teeth, sweeping claws, and Daisy's stop-sign post.

Tara clapped her palms over her face. "Here come more."

Vick had stopped counting how many of Ms. Alba's eight groups of five watchdogs had come through the breach. Now he saw that it had only been six—she'd kept two in reserve. They swarmed around the wall and charged the hill.

Daisy broke away and angled down the hill. Half of Ms. Alba's fresh troops split off to go after Daisy as Tara's spider dropped from its hiding place onto the back of a charging wolf. It bit a hunk out of its neck.

"Eighteen," Tara said.

Daisy was moving more slowly. One of her hind legs looked mangled, and she'd lost one of her eyes. There must have been ten watchdogs chasing her, the grizzly in the lead. It was banged up but still moving well.

Daisy reached the base of the building where Vick and the rest were hiding and turned, her back to the wall so nothing could sneak up on her.

Ms. Alba's watchdogs charged, all at once. Daisy skewered the first three that reached her, then shielded herself from snapping teeth and flashing blades by keeping the body of the biggest, a piggish-looking thing, between her and her attackers.

"Thirteen," Tara whispered when Daisy's jaws snapped down on the face of the turtle-watchdog with the clubbed tail. There were five watchdogs battling Daisy, which meant there were eight more out in the rubble, fighting the other survivors from their little army.

One of the smaller watchdogs had clawed its way

behind Daisy. It wrapped itself around one of her hind legs and bit repeatedly, searching for a weak spot. The weight of the watchdog made Daisy stumble. The grizzly took advantage, bounding over the top of the watchdog wreckage Daisy was using as a shield and sinking its teeth into her shoulder.

Daisy surged backward and slammed the raccoon-sized watchdog clinging to her leg into the wall. It fell to the ground, badly damaged.

The grizzly slashed wildly at Daisy's face with its long claws, catching Daisy's good eye and raking it.

Beside Vick, Tara froze. "Oh no. Oh no, Daisy."

Daisy flailed at the grizzly with the pole. The grizzly broke away and backed off a few steps.

Daisy turned in one direction, then another, swinging the pole, trying to keep the watchdogs away, but she had no idea where they were. She was blind.

The grizzly waited for Daisy to swing the pole, then lunged and hit her, denting the side of her head. It backed away just as Daisy swung the pole. One of the other surviving watchdogs, a velociraptor, scraped a foot along the concrete to Daisy's left; when she turned and swung in the direction of the sound, the grizzly struck again, deepening the dent in her head.

Tara tried to stand, but Vick pulled her back down.

"We have to help her."

"How are we going to do that?" His voice was thick with emotion. It was killing him to see Daisy smashed up by those things down there. And before long those things would be searching for *them*.

The grizzly hit Daisy again. Daisy fell. She tried to get her legs under her but fell over again. The grizzly landed one more savage blow to her head, then reached down and began peeling back the armor at her hind end.

"It's looking for the chip," East said.

Little Daisy ejected and tried to run, but the grizzly's paw came down on her, pinning her to the ground. Still holding her down, it picked her up in its teeth.

"Daisy!" Tara shouted.

Everyone shushed her.

"There's nothing we can—" Vick froze. He looked around at the debris scattered all around. A chunk of concrete the size of a backpack was perched near the edge.

Vick slapped Rando on the arm. "Help me." They had to be quick, before the grizzly moved away.

Vick grabbed one end of the chunk of concrete, and Rando the other. Gasping with the effort, they carried it to the edge.

"On three," Vick said. They rocked it twice, gauging the distance, and let it go.

The concrete landed dead center on the grizzly's

back, driving it to the ground like a car T-boning an eighteen-wheeler.

Little Daisy wriggled out of the grizzly's mouth and ran right for Tara's spider, which broke off from its fight with a giant beetle and raced to meet her. Daisy jumped onto the spider's back, and they headed for higher ground with five of Ms. Alba's watchdogs close behind. Vick spotted a lone wolf running to meet them, with a big panther and a snaggle-toothed wolverine on her heels. Seven against two and a half.

"Oh no," Rando said. Vick followed his gaze.

The gorilla watchdog was looking up at them.

Not seven. Eight.

It headed for the stairs.

East picked up a chunk of concrete. "Find something to fight with. Anything."

His heart hammering in his ears, Vick scanned the littered floor. All the chunks looked too big or too small. Not that it mattered. Police with guns backed down from fights with watchdogs; how could he and his friends win against them with just . . . *rocks*? Was there anywhere they could run? Vick looked around. There was no way up, no way down but the stairs.

"Vick!" Torch tossed him a piece of two-by-four.

Vick caught it with two hands. "What are you going to use?"

Torch held up his portable laser cutter and smiled. Vick couldn't imagine how Torch could get close enough to the gorilla to cut it without being killed, but it was something. It was a chance.

The gorilla stopped at the top of the stairs, like it was soaking in the moment. It looked right at Tara.

Vick couldn't believe she wasn't curled up in the corner shrieking for someone to make it go away. She was standing there, a chunk of concrete in her hand, looking right at the thing. Vick was terrified, but he also felt so proud of her. He wouldn't let that thing hurt her.

"I'm so proud of you," he said. "You're not just smart, you're brave."

"Shut up and concentrate," Tara said.

The gorilla charged Tara.

He wouldn't let it get to her. He wouldn't. Vick raised the two-by-four and ran right at the charging gorilla.

As they came together, the gorilla swung its huge fist.

Vick opened his eyes. He was on the ground, his head aching like he'd never felt it ache before. The gorilla loomed over him, iron fist raised.

Rando leaped and wrapped his arms and legs around the gorilla's raised arm. East and Tara swung chunks of concrete, slamming them down on the gorilla's head like they were hammering nails. North was pounding its back with a rock the size of his own head. Then Torch was on the gorilla's back, the laser cutter in his hand. He got to work on the gorilla's neck.

The gorilla shook itself and swung its free arm, buffeting Torch, but Torch hung on. It turned its attention back to Vick and opened its mouth, exposing a row of sharp, triangular fangs. Tara shrieked and wrapped her arms around that huge head as it came down. Its fangs snapped closed an inch from Vick's face.

Another set of hands—Rando's—appeared around the gorilla's face as it strained to reach Vick, its jaws snapping with a metallic clank.

The head began to bend up, away from Vick's face.

Suddenly it snapped free from the gorilla's neck and dropped onto Vick's chest, knocking the wind out of him.

East rolled it off and the others helped him out from under the gorilla's headless body.

"You all right?" Rando asked.

Gasping, staggering to his feet, Vick nodded. After having the gorilla's fangs so close to his face, the ache in his chest felt good in comparison. He followed the others as they ran to the edge to see what was happening.

The wolf was gone. The spider was in bad shape. Daisy was still on top of it, their backs to the wall directly below Vick and his friends, surrounded by Ms.

Alba's last four watchdogs. Daisy had led the enemy back to the only troops she had left: them.

"Go. Go. Go. Go." Tara grabbed a brick lying beside her.

Vick squatted in front of a big chunk of concrete and then deadlifted it, the rough stone scraping his palms as the others ran to find something to drop.

His toes poking over the edge, Vick swung the concrete chunk between his legs and let it go. Losing his balance, he windmilled his arms as he tipped forward, his stomach lurching.

A hand locked on the back of his shirt.

"*Whoa,*" Torch said, yanking him back.

The concrete chunk slammed into the beetle's head, taking it right off. The thing collapsed in a heap.

The panther went down a moment later. They took aim on the two remaining watchdogs, raining bricks and fist-sized chunks of concrete down on them.

When the last was down, Daisy took off on the spider.

"Where is she going?" Rando asked.

"To get Ms. Alba," Tara said.

Vick could see Ms. Alba running for her Maserati. He could also see that she wasn't going to make it.

CHAPTER 21

They stood amid the mangled wreckage of what had been Ms. Alba's sweatshop as the spider finished turning everything inside the inner office to scrap metal, firewood, and confetti. All her captive workers were gone, free to return to their families. Ms. Alba was trying to act as if the destruction of her empire was no big deal, but her forehead was shining with sweat, and as she swiped a wisp of hair from her eyes, her hand was shaking badly.

Dixie and Stripe looked flat-out scared. They probably weren't sure if Vick was going to have the spider do to them what it was doing to the sweatshop. He would never hurt someone, no matter how much they deserved it, but he was in no hurry to let *them* know that.

"Are we through here?" Ms. Alba asked when the spider clicked out of the office. Her voice was higher than usual.

"Not quite," Vick said. Daisy appeared from inside the office, carrying a plastic bag in her mouth. Inside were three tubes containing tracker syringes.

Ms. Alba took a step back. "Wait a minute. We both know those can be deactivated."

"Sure, once you locate the proper equipment." East accepted the bag from Daisy and handed out the syringes. Ms. Alba hesitated for a long moment but finally plucked it from East's hand as if it were a dead rat.

"Go on," Vick said. "You've all had plenty of practice giving those shots. Now you'll see how it feels."

Ms. Alba, Dixie, and Stripe all studied the syringes they were holding, looking like they'd just eaten something rotten.

"Or Torch can do it for you," Vick said.

"You definitely don't want me to do it for you," Torch said, looking on with his arms folded across his chest.

Stripe reached across and stuck the needle into his shoulder. He let out a long, slow breath as he pressed the plunger.

Dixie cursed under her breath, then squeezed her eyes shut. She inhaled sharply as the needle bit.

Everyone turned to Ms. Alba. She held her syringe out to Dixie. "I hate needles. You do it."

"I did mine, you can do yours," Dixie snapped.

Ms. Alba held the syringe out to Stripe.

Stripe raised his hands. "Not a chance. I told you to forget about the chip and leave that watchdog alone. But did you listen? No. You had to push it."

Torch stepped forward and held out his hand. "Here, I'll do it."

Ms. Alba jerked the syringe out of his reach. "All right. I'll do it." She raised the syringe. "I hate needles." She squeezed her eyes shut and plunged the needle in.

When she was finished, she flung the empty syringe to the floor.

"You've got thirty minutes to get out of Chicago," East said. "If you're not gone, our friend here will come after you."

All three headed for the door.

When they were gone, Vick and his friends stood silently in the sweatshop office. A tightness that had been in Vick's chest for so long he hadn't realized it was there suddenly loosened. He took a few smooth, easy breaths, relishing the sensation.

"So what do we do now?" Rando asked, looking around at the wreckage.

"First, we make Daisy a new body," Tara said.

"And after that?" Rando asked.

It was a good question. Now that Ms. Alba was gone, they were free to use Daisy to earn enough to rent a safe place to live and have enough to eat, but Vick was back to wondering exactly how to do that.

"I have an idea," East said.

CHAPTER 22

*U*nderdressed was too weak a word for what Vick felt as they rose in the spotless glass elevator, shifting left and right with the contours of the skyscraper. His clothes no longer stank, but they were nothing more than rags covering his skin.

He examined his friends and felt slightly better. They all looked just as bad, except for Daisy with her shiny new body, made from parts salvaged from the watch-dogs defeated in the final showdown.

"Remember," Vick said to Daisy, "you're just a dumb watchdog. You're only here to model; we don't want any-one to suspect we have something that might belong to the military."

Daisy nodded.

"I still don't understand how you thought to get in touch with a patent lawyer," Torch said to East. "How did you even know what a patent lawyer *was*? I never heard of it before."

East caught Vick's eye and smiled. "Something I learned about in a past life."

The waiting room was all granite and chrome; a miniature waterfall cascaded down the center, through stones that seemed to defy gravity. A guy in a dark suit who'd been messing with his fancy phone gaped at Daisy as they entered, the phone sliding out of his hand and dropping to the seat cushion beside him.

After less than five minutes, the guy, who turned out to be the receptionist, led them into a big room with a long black conference table down the middle. A woman and a man, both dressed in crisp, perfect suits, were waiting. They introduced themselves as Camille Hernandez and Rolfe Weiss, then went right over to check out Daisy.

"Oh my goodness," Rolfe said, his voice hushed. "I was excited from the photos, but I had no idea. This is magnificent."

"Thank you," Tara said.

"Look at this." Camille pointed at Daisy's eye. "Is this a three-hundred-sixty-degree design?"

Tara nodded. "I'm very good at designing watchdogs."

"I'll say," Camille replied, running a finger across Daisy's hip.

Daisy gave Vick a look, as if to say, *Am I acting dumb enough for you?* Vick just smiled at her.

"You designed her all by yourself?" Rolfe asked Tara.

"That's right," Tara said.

After a few minutes of this, Camille straightened, then looked at Rolfe. "Have you seen enough?"

"More than enough."

Camille turned to Tara. "We'd like to represent you. I can see a dozen patentable innovations just from this quick examination. Our firm gets fifteen percent, which is standard. East said you want to find investors, rather than sell the patents outright?"

Tara looked at East. "Is that what I want?"

East nodded. "That means you're going into business for yourself."

Tara nodded emphatically. "That's what I want."

"It complicates things that you're minors without legal guardians, but in these times I think we can work around that, given what you're bringing to the table."

Camille offered her hand to Tara. "Do we have a deal?"

East stopped Tara's hand before she could shake. "You want one more thing."

"What's that?"

East looked Camille right in the eye and said, "She needs ten thousand dollars, right now."

Camille blinked. "Oh. You mean, start-up funding?"

East pointed at her. "Exactly. That."

Camille looked at Rolfe, who shrugged. She nodded. "We can do that."

Vick felt an asthma attack coming on. He also thought he was going to faint. Ten thousand dollars.

"I'll be right back with a contract and a cashier's check." Camille whisked out of the room with Rolfe on her heels. They looked excited. That was extremely cool, that a couple of patent lawyers were excited about representing them.

"Hey." Rando put a hand on Vick's shoulder. "Can we, like, work for you? I know you don't need us, that you can hire pros now, but since we're friends and all . . ."

Vick burst out laughing. "You stood between me and a guy who was going to drag me back to Alba to collect a bounty." He looked at Torch. "And you. You helped me cut up the bot who took my mother's job, then you cut up a killer watchdog whose fangs were an inch from my face. You're not friends. You're family." He choked up, blinking back tears. It seemed like it had been forever since Vick had trusted anyone besides Tara. It felt good to let a few more people in.

He looked at Tara, who nodded in agreement. "You got that straight. This is our company. All of us."

Torch let out a whoop that caused half a dozen people in the hallway to look in at them through the glass wall. He covered his mouth and called, "Sorry."

"Can we get an apartment now?" Tara asked. "With royal blue carpet and shell tile in the kitchen? And a white concrete birdbath in the backyard in the corner by the water recycler?"

"We sure can." Vick held up a finger. "But first we're going to get some quesadillas, and some corn on the cob, and chocolate milk."

"That sounds good," East said. "I'm starving."

"Or we could send your dumb watchdog out to get it," Torch said, grinning.

Laughing, Tara wrapped her arms around Daisy and gave her a fierce hug, then kissed her steel cheek.

Daisy just stood there, playing dumb.

ACKNOWLEDGMENTS

Watchdog grew out of an email conversation with Kate Sullivan, my editor at Delacorte Press. We were batting around ideas for my next young adult book, and I tossed out the idea for *Watchdog*. She said it seemed like a great idea for a book for middle-grade kids. That stuck with me, because I wanted to write a middle-grade book—a book my own kids would be old enough to read right about the time it came out. I wouldn't have written *Watchdog* if not for that spark from Kate. Plus, Kate liked the result enough to publish *Watchdog*, and made it a better book through her insightful editing, so I'm triply grateful to her.

Many thanks to Laurel Amberdine and Jessi Cole

Jackson (fellow YA/MG authors and Codex Writers' Group members), who critiqued the first draft of *Watchdog*, and to my longtime brainstorming partner, Jim Pugh, who helped me get unstuck time and again as I wrote that first draft.

Before I run with an idea, I've taken to testing it out on Jacob Robinson, who works in Hollywood (now with TBS). He (kindly and constructively) shoots down most of the ideas I send him, but *Watchdog* he loved. His enthusiasm got me enthused; he made a few crucial suggestions to the original two-sentence idea I sent him, and that was the start of what became this book. Thank you, Jacob!

Thanks also to my agent, Seth Fishman. He and I have been a team since my first novel was published seven years ago. He was an early fan of *Watchdog*, as well as the person who first got me to think about writing for readers of different ages.

Finally, gratitude and love to my family and friends. To my wife, Alison; to our dynamic duo, Miles and Hannah; to my parents and sister and her family; to Aunt M and Aunt Jane; to my in-laws, Bill and Ginny Scott; to my sister-in-law, Liz, and her family; and to my friends Beau, Saul, Colin & Jeannie, Tony & David, Mike, Larry, Suzanne & David, Lenny, Ted, Sara, and many others who have let me bounce ideas off them, encouraged me, supported me. Thank you all.

ABOUT THE AUTHOR

Will McIntosh is the author of several adult speculative fiction novels and a frequent short-story writer. His first novel, *Soft Apocalypse,* was a finalist for the Locus Award. "Bridesicle," a short story published in *Asimov's Science Fiction,* won a Hugo Award for Best Short Story and was later expanded into his novel *Love Minus Eighty,* which was an ALA-RUSA Reading List Selection for Science Fiction. His most recent novel for adults, *Defenders,* has been optioned for film by Warner Bros. Will is also the author of *Burning Midnight,* his first novel for young adults. He lives with his wife and twin children in Williamsburg, Virginia.